TEST DRIVE

a novel

PATRICK McGINTY

PROPELLER BOOKS

PORTLAND, OREGON • UNITED STATES OF AMERICA

TEST DRIVE

"Cities controlled by companies are old hat in science fiction... The company-city subgenre always seemed to star a hero who outsmarted, overthrew, or escaped 'the company'..."
—Octavia Butler, *The Parable of the Sower*

PART I
October 15th, 2030

1

HUNTING IN THE BLUEGILL

RIGHT TURNS are a pain. Any test driver knows this. Right turns lead to trouble. They lead to water. Where a left turn safely escorts a driver through a crowned intersection, a right turn lowers them, topographically.

Right turns suck.

They suck at six a.m. They suck in ancient neighborhoods that have known nineteenth-century hooves. Right turns suck in pretty much all of potholed Pittsburgh, a city which answers the question: what would it look like if we paved the moon? The potholes threaten test drivers and also real drivers, on those pesky right turns and also lefts, the latter of which, to hear Janice Pegula tell it, are actually quite kind. Left turns reel a driver in. They offer the driver an excessively padded center console. A right turn is when a driverless car really levels with a driver about its intentions. A right turn shoves a driver toward the door.

At six a.m., Janice—she is "Pegs" to her friends—switches from *Mechanic* to *Test Driver* in Revo's HR app, types a personal or prescribed destination into a driverless prototype, and then she and whichever model she's piloting start making right turns through swampy corners and small city ponds. The first one on Wednesday is dark and flat. It is also immediate, stretching across the entirety of the exit out of Revo's lot. The BlueGill Pegs is test driving—BlueGill3, four-door, lidar-directed, recently waxed— is unafraid of the wide pool. The car has a destination and a turn to make. The steering wheel rotates without her input. Halfway through the puddle, the wheel respools itself.

The next right turn is trickier. The puddle is thick with mud, and the BlueGill's tires fight. When it exits onto visible asphalt, the splash sneezes across the intersection, a murky firework— then the vehicle drops. The front left wheel splatters into a pothole. The bumper hits, scrapes, and recovers. It's the kind of quick drop that Pegs can feel in her molars, though at present, her problem is not Revo's iffy dental for contract employees. Her problem concerns the brief rattle in the trunk. The metallic noise is not strictly car-related. It seems much more related to the items Pegs has transferred from the Revo supply room. Some part or box back there has fallen. Worse, some item is now possibly broken.

Instinctually, Pegs coughs. There's a mic buried in the rear view mirror, a camera in the dash. She stares through the windshield. She has honed an approach for moments like these, when she fears that the driver monitoring system has got the goods on her: emit polite noise, then become a deer on a calendar.

The BlueGill buys it. The monitoring system does not stop the route due to the *tink-tink-tink* in the trunk. It doesn't treat her yawny cough as being worthy of an Inattentive. There's no second rattle or clatter, just the airy hum of the electric engine that accelerates or brakes depending on feedback from radar sensors above the headlights. The whirling lidar sensor on the roof has a major say, too, though apparently the pothole upgrade needs work. Pegs is very much the type of employee who still says *upgrade*. Other employees now say *customization*, sometimes *affirmation*. She never participates in the AV sector's endless language games. She still struggles to explain whether the prototypes are *driverless* or *self-driven*, *automated* or *autonomous*, *robo*, who knows.

What Pegs knows is that various aspects of the cars still need upgrades, hence the need for more test routes. The screen blinks. It alerts her to an upcoming left.

This particular left is unusual. The intersection is not clear and dry. The BlueGill turns, and before the the headlights can find the new lane, they light a truly monstrous puddle. It spans the entire intersection and holds a mini-neighborhood of plastic trash. Pegs sees the tall gallon of iced tea and thinks: great views, sturdy foundation, available November 1st. A plastic bag is curled like the ridiculous indoor hammock she saw on some apartment listing in either Squirrel Hill or Troy Hill. She is driven slowly past bobbing quarts and Cokes. They topple and drift off before her apartment-addled mind can compare the plastic to some listing she's seen a hundred times.

When she glances up at Polish Hill, she can't help wondering if there are new apartment listings up there. The neighborhood is on her radar. There's more doable, potential options for her there than in newer neighborhoods. Unfortunately, scrolling a phone is very much not doable for test drivers when they're on duty. It is technically doable, but it's dangerous, more so career-wise than anything road-related. The cars disengage whenever the monitoring system spots phone usage. Headquarters tends to call, though not always. It would be safer to simply punch in a new destination in Polish Hill. Some realtors still hang signs.

The advice Pegs often gives herself in these antsy moments is this: just fix your hands on your lap and get to where you've already decided to go. Her thinking is that if she keeps her hands still, her mind will follow.

Like pretty much all things related to driverless cars, this hand-mind thing is more a nice theory than a functional habit. Her hands are still for five seconds, maybe ten. Within a block, she is scratching her gray rain jacket that's long enough to be a company-sponsored night gown. She tells herself to simply watch as the city comes awake, but she doesn't process the two- and three-story Strip District warehouses, the emergent rain, the glowing jogger. There's nothing notable or worrisome on the screen, and so her mind begins to scroll a different one. More specifically: her mind is on Rūm, the apartment-finding app she has been using for almost a week. She has already determined the notification system is for losers. Living on the app is the only way to beat others to the listings. If even one Pittsburgh realtor is up early, hustling and posting, it will justify a quick glance, and a glance might be all it takes to finally move.

She needs a higher apartment. She needs it soon.

She has been saving. Saving is probably not what her coworkers would call the situation in the trunk. Fortunately, they tend to stay busy debating other terms. The car, on the other hand, is tougher to deceive. It's like having a loyal sidekick and a micro-managing boss all on one dashboard. The hardest part of using her phone while test driving is getting it from her pocket to her thigh. A sloth could quick-draw a pistol faster than Pegs removes her phone. Once she's on Rūm, though, she's fast. She knows the interface cold and can assess apartments without moving her face or neck. It's like her thumb has irises. The top listings are old. Old in this market means a day. The only real possibility is the second-floor unit in Garfield. It meets certain standards of hers, namely: it's a second floor. The problem is that the apartment is high in price, too. It's as though the realtor tacked on an extra hundred for every foot that the windows are above a sewer drain.

She knows what will happen if her thumb changes the filter from "Second-Floor" to "All." She does it anyway. Cheap basement apartments flood the screen. She's seen them all, on her test drives and on three separate apps. None of the basements are better or safer than the one she currently shares with her sister. It strikes her that none are worth the daily fee she's paying for Rūm's premium access. The day's charge is due at 6:20.

Pegs presses her thumb to the screen, hard. There are better ways to spend money. She likes Twix bars. If she cut the daily fee for a whole month, she could rent a shop vac for when a surge fills their apartment.

Her phone does not like these plans. It shudders on her lap, ruffling her whole jacket. When she glances down, her phone informs her that app deletion cannot occur without confirmation. Rūm wants reasons. The questions are phrased strangely, specifically the bit about identifying what is responsible for her unhappiness. How could she even—

Red light fills the car. Pegs raises her eyes and covers her phone with the sleeves of her rain jacket, but she's too late. Words blink on the console screen. Their ruby glow makes the letters bleed together as the BlueGill brakes, hard. The seat belt bites her chest. The bags and boxes in the trunk collide. They crash into the car frame, into what sounds like church bells, into timpanis, plus a wreath of toilets, God it's loud. The prototype must have made a wicked tire squeal, but Pegs wouldn't know. The supplies in the trunk are still clattering. She overpacked.

Her eyes open. She withdraws her hand from the back of her

neck. None of the trunk's contents are lodged in her skull. None are strewn across the roomy backseat, viewable to a passerby, be they human or drone. The words on the screen blink. Their redness fashions the car a mobile hell, an oven on wet, robotized wheels. The alert reads: DISENGAGED—INATTENTIVE.

2

INCOMING

THE AVERAGE test ride is something like 2.6 hours. The screen informs her that she had only been driving seven minutes before the Inattentive. Seven minutes is bad. It's worse than bad. Seven minutes isn't even enough to change neighborhoods. The BlueGill had started in the new part of the Strip District, where lofts and tech companies occupy huge river warehouses that once made cotton, cork, and ketchup; the vehicle now idles in the old-world part of the Strip, where merchants still go outdoors. A store owner is raising a metal grate. Boys and one girl haul out tables beneath the rain tents. They slam the legs on the walk like they're planting flags on some drizzly planet.

On screen, the disengagement alert disappears and is replaced by:

Incoming: Revo HQ
Janice Pegula: Accept?

Pegs clears her throat, answers. "Nothing technical," she says, "disregard." She instructs herself not to yawn.

"Was it phone or fatigue?" The caller himself sounds fatigued and then some. Safety supervisories can be done remotely from 8pm to 8am, meaning staffers always call from home. She can't tell whether the sluggish voice is Dellinger or Yabner. Every Revo guy sounds the same—driven and smart, but perpetually tired, even more so at dawn. Revo guys project confidence but, like their autonomous vehicles, only in select, carefully-controlled environments.

Unfortunately, a safety call is one such environment. Pegs debates a joke to lighten the mood. Or: she could mother the guy, tell him he sounds beat, get some rest, he's got a big day ahead. "I'm fine alone," she ends up saying. "I'm going to eat, then drive."

"You're only eight blocks away." There's clicking. It's unclear if the sound is typing or mouth-related. If it's Dellinger, he's scrolling her file to count her Inattentives. If it's Yabner, he's sucking the seedy bits from one of his special smoothies he's always drinking, which look like the machines in the caf figured out how to repurpose the swarms of bugs from the rising rivers.

"Geez, Pegs." The caller is one thousand percent Dellinger. Yabner or Smith or pretty much anyone else would not express sympathy after being awakened at six-fifteen. "I'm showing you conducted test drives from seven to ten last night then performed maintenance on the fleet."

"I'm behind on road hours," Pegs says.

"Are you in need of assistance?"

"It's a little late to ask."

There's a yawn, more clicking. Dellinger wakes up. It's like he's starting the call over. "Do you need a vehicle recovery?"

"Negative."

"Fuel?"

"You can ditch the script."

"What about dental implants?" he says. "Flood and surge insurance?"

There's times where it pays to joke around, to suck up, bond. This is not one of those times. Pegs needs to get moving. The store owner is making unfriendly eyes. He's standing guard over his rain jackets.

"I'll be in later," she tells Dellinger.

"I'll list it as fatigue."

"I appreciate it."

"It's not that I care." Another sign it's Dellinger: Yabner would never invoke care. "But I'm seeing that if you log one more Inattentive of any sort, you're probably looking at a re-train."

"Not happening."

"I know it's a lot going from the garage to the road."

She terminates the call. The console screen is temporarily blank. BlueGill3 asks: *Continue Route?*

She affirms with a finger. She needs a separate button to kick-start her eyeballs. They feel top-heavy. Her head? Heavy as a lead-acid car battery.

The automated departure helps. They're never smooth. She jolts forward. The car hits five miles per hour, seven. For half a block, the rain is faster than the BlueGill. It's like she's on an amusement ride, an old one, a wooden coaster initiated by some zitty teen. No phone, no phone, she thinks. She can deal with another daily charge for the app. She tells herself she'll delete it later. She tells herself that there won't be super awesome apartments listed at six-twenty-six a.m. Nor six-twenty-three. On a rainy right turn it feels like her skin is wrapped around the hood. A pile of bricks and a garbage can are so incredibly close, too close, and so she reclines what is allowable.

Blinking red dots speed past overhead.

She switches the view to aerial—it's delivery drones. There's a steady stream of them, out early, in force, though you wouldn't necessarily know it from the console screen. For a company whose entire business pivot is 'surge safety via unparalleled aerially reinforced sight,' the BlueGill's screen broadcasts a pretty shoddy rendering of the drones. Their lights don't show up well. Nor do the suctions lining their spidery arms. On screen, the drones and their dangly packages look like two-celled organisms speeding through lava, like they're entities with kidneys and writhing blood vessels as opposed to wires and engines. She's not positive that drones do in fact have engines. Despite working in autonomous vehicles for two years, she knows shockingly little about automation at-large. She doesn't know what to call the massive construction machine above and beside her on the Bloomfield Bridge.

An auto-excavator?

An AI-hoe?

The huge yellow machine lacks a driver. This isn't much of an issue, seeing as the machine doesn't seem to move more than two miles an hour. The beastly thing has parked itself against the thick concrete side of the bridge. Its two circular blades rev, spark. They're cutting a rectangular hole into the barrier. Some sort of suction or grip mechanism she can't see yanks the human-sized slab to the bridge. Water spills out of the emergency drainage hole. A guy in a hard hat leans over the short wall, grading the style and arc of the overflow onto the railroad tracks in the ravine. The other workers are attaching a metal piece of guard rail across the previous incision, one of maybe ten. From below, there's no observable pattern to where the machine has carved out drainage. It looks like the workers are wrangling braces onto a concrete ogre.

She passes the dentist and the Thai place with the good toothpicks. The BlueGill parks at its destination: the laundromat. The screen asks: *Where To?*

It takes a minute or two for Pegs to transform BlueGill3 into a normal, untrackable car. Mostly untrackable, at any rate. She turns off the BlueGill, then starts it. She opts for manual instead of automated, pressing *Yes* twice, *No* once. Disabling the driver monitoring system is trickier. She has to opt out of each safety feature individually—the camera watching her face from

the steering column, the mic, some temperate gauge thing that
seems completely made up. Before canceling each feature, she
has to confirm that she intends to drive manually and that the
onus is on her. Logging out of the GPS system has more to do
with karma than stealth. There's a physical GPS tracker on each
prototype, though their logs are checked about as often as the
front window is cleaned at the unpronounceable Lil' Italy Laundry. The trackers are mostly for locating a vehicle in the event of
a software-destroying crash.

In manual, she departs her parking spot on Liberty Avenue.
She rounds a corner, rolls a stop sign, then slips into the alley.
Lester's Auto has never shown up in the BlueGill's system. It
never will, nor will she ever let a driverless prototype safari lane-
lessly in his alley. You have to know which potholes are shallow
and which have been up late chugging two feet of soft rain.
She aims the tires astride The Hole to China. She plays chicken
with the uprooted basketball hoop. Its big steroidal clump of
concrete is dying to cobweb a headlight. You couldn't draw up a
less surge-proof item: stand-alone, top-heavy, thin.

Lester's tow is low and heavy. She pulls alongside it and honks
at the double garage door. Rain responds. It picks up. It's too
dark to tell what kind of October day it will be. It's raining normal rain. There's no violence to it. They've got four weeks, maybe
five.

She revs. Bags shift in the trunk. The teeny lone items scatter,
rattle, maybe break. The boxes thud and hold. Like a slow gray
curtain, the garage door rises.

3

THE BUYER

THE GARAGE lowers behind her. She pops the trunk, gets out. Lester crosses his arms. "I told you—I don't want you parking these robot cars in my shop."

"It's raining."

"That's a five hundred dollar rain jacket they give you."

"This stuff's heavy." Pegs raises the trunk. She hands Lester a garbage bag—shock absorbers. She stands up the tall yellow box of windshield wipers. The fan belts she stacks on the box are leftovers from when the fleet ran on gas. The pile of supplies looks like some kind of bow-and-arrow, hook-and-line contraption that'll lasso down every last delivery drone.

Lester runs the belts through his fingers. He prods the box of wipers with his disgusting shoe. Is his shoe brown? Black? Burned? The shoe is a letter a Minuteman wrote to his mum about how muddy the barracks are. Lester himself looks like a guy whose first job in vehicles was hammering horseshoes onto thoroughbreds in Valley Forge or Concord or whatever muck-hole a bunch of idealists were squatting in, rent-free. It's not even seven a.m. yet, and his forearms and hands are filmed with grime. He's hunchy, but you can tell by the way he lifts the box of wipers that he's still got hop, a short wrestler with one good go in him. The windshield wipers aren't worth the tussle. He drops the box. His face: a perpetual fight between a grin and pout. "It'll take a month to move all these wipers."

"Make a surge special."

"I don't use this brand."

Pegs checks the apartment app. The three-thousand-dollars-a-month apartment in Garfield is still the newest listing. She closes Rūm and hops onto Lester's low workbench. Eighty-five metal items rattle. Eighty-five screens ask her to authenticate the LedgerCoin account she shares with Lester. Rain hammers the metal awning outside. It's annoying, relentless. She can't remember how she ever dealt with it all day.

"I been killing rats on that bench." Lester points. The detour in his finger has gotten better. This is because she's thinking of his other hand. "Right where you're sitting."

"Liar." It might actually be true. The work bench looks like four toddlers beat the surface with forks until they were teenagers. It could be claws. The deer on the calendar says: I didn't see nothing.

Lester confesses that he's been killing rats wherever he finds them. They're all over, he says. They run uphill. "They feel those surges. They're coming."

"Did you seriously only send fifty bucks?" Pegs holds up her screen like it's a badge, he's arrested, *you have the right*, one call.

Lester removes his glasses. He looks through them. He cleans them above his crotch. "Those were good bearings."

"And hub assemblies."

"The only way I compete," Lester tells her, "is price."

"We're going to drown if we can't afford a higher apartment."

"You feed too many." Lester pauses to interpret thunder. It's low, soft—not a surge yet. Could be a rolling tire parting garbage. Could be rolling garbage parting tires. "Tell the blonde I'm calling the cops next time she carries batteries through the front."

Lester transports the belts and wires in separate hands. Pegs returns to her phone. She relives their transactions. Forty-five dollars, twenty dollars, fifty dollars: it's not much. It reads like fees. It's like a list of surge-maintenance tack-ons the utilities will start charging her. "This isn't working," she tells Lester.

"It's working exactly."

Pegs slides off the workbench and reaches inside the proto-type. Showing off all the machinery the BlueGill has in the area where most other electric vehicles have a front trunk is against four or five hundred sections of her NDA, and she triggers the hood faster than a driver monitoring system chirping *Janice Pegs Pegula, you are looking for second- and third-floor apartments on your test drive.* Lester tells her to knock it off.

"There's got to be a bigger play," she says.

Lester assesses his work bench. He finds a flathead. He ignores the car and its naked engine. He tilts the box of wipers and runs the blade across the tape. "Your people put trackers on their balls."

"What's this *your* people?" Pegs says as she props the hood. No single part glows with meaning, revelation, easy detachable profit. The car never breaks thirty-five. It exercises its brake pads only when Pegs nods off after a night-long maintenance shift. Nothing is ever wrong, let alone detachable. "What if I misdiagnosed a gasket or something. I could get them to order a new tranny then bring you the good original."

Lester lifts a quiver of wipers from the box. He says it's a lot of risk for a little profit. She begs him to scan the car.

"It's a car." Lester stuffs the wipers on a shelf. They look fishy in their plastic sleeves. None of the fans or tubes she brought came with rainjackets. The two long overhead lights flicker. "I know what's in there."

A hollow object rebounds off the metal garage door. Pegs

tenses. No other noise follows. Rain on the awning: that's it. She watches the side door. No one enters.

"Don't tell me you're one of these panickers," Lester says.

"Surges could come early."

"Everybody's a shaman." Lester crosses his arms over the BlueGill. It's like he's looking at a painting one of his fifty grandkids did of him. The rendering is overweight, armless, gray. He points at the roof. "Sell one of these laser eyes if you're so desperate. The eight-wheel people would pay for a look."

"Six."

"I counted eight whole wheels yesterday."

Peg hops back onto the workbench and explains that Ryde uses six wheels, not eight. And, in the same way that Revo couldn't do much with an extra wheel suspension from Ryde, Ryde couldn't do much with a special lidar helmet from Revo. Same goes for Norroyo's cameras. Pegs underhands a washer at the lidar helmet riding on BlueGill3's roof. It's like a massive crown. The washer clinks off the clear protective shell.

Lester paces between the workbench and the car. The lidar, which usually spins like an all-seeing over-caffeinated carousel, is dormant inside its clear helmet. It's a black yolk inside a clear shell, an egg from a Moon ostrich that mated with a jellyfish from Mars. Lester tests the lidar frame with his hands. He taps the protective helmet. "The surges they're talking about this year," he says, "will blow this bike rack to kingdom come."

"They're going to find my apartment in that kingdom."

Lester asks how much is left in Revo's supply room. Pegs waffles her hand. She allows herself a yawn. It makes her stomach twice as empty. She tries to picture her last meal and can't. She tries to picture an appealing breakfast anywhere in her kitchen. God willing, her sister shopped.

The long fluorescents above the BlueGill fizz out. They come back. It's hard to tell whether it's the light, the building, the weather. She doesn't want to play guessing games. She wants to level. "What's the best way to make some real money? Fast."

"Quit letting the other girls drop parts. Cut 'em," Lester says. When she doesn't respond, he says, "You can't run holding hands."

Pegs assembles screws. With a thumb, she carousels them in her palm. "It's not that I disagree."

"Robots and rain," Lester says. "They're coming."

"News at ten."

A light flickers, holds. Lester watches it. "You sure you can't sell the roof gizmos?" he says.

"Tried." Sort of. Leah talked to avatars in car and tech forums. Most buyers just wanted pictures. Of Leah. Pegs flips another washer. It sails over the lidar helmet. "We should've been doing this back when they were scrapping their cars every ten thousand miles."

"These people wonder why they're short on cash."

Thunder oozes down the alley. It's a car. It hits the Hole to China. Either that, or it hit the tow. Above her, the long light blinks. On the calendar, the deer's dots shine like a brown plate of glow-in-the-dark teeth. They stay burned in her vision. "Give me seventy-five for the hub assembly."

Lester gets on tiptoe at the door. He peeks through the high window. He says it's really raining, that the surges are coming, any day, he can feel it. He says Revo shouldn't have asked her to drive. It's too much, what with her mechanic's duties. And in surges? Criminal.

"There's no money in cars that pull over in a storm," she tells him.

"It's all a bucket of smoke." Lester transfer wipers to a higher shelf. "Empty shoes."

She closes her palm and rattles the screws like prickly dice. There's a whole fight she doesn't want to rehash.

Him: They exploit you.

Her: Why do you think we're pilfering the supply room?

Him: Quit.

Her: Do you want stats on jobs lost to automation?

Him: Be yours pretty soon. Me, too.

Her: Hence the pilfer.

Him: Just play your threes and fours right, then they'll bump you to a service center.

Her: They'll just pair up with national chains.

Him: I never exploited you.

Her: You could barely pay. And I cleaned. Everything. Always.

She tidies the pile of screws she disrupted. She nods toward the trunk and asks why he didn't take the seat belts.

"Who doesn't have seat belts," he says. "Nobody wants inflatables."

"These are rare." She lifts them. They're like snakes that have popped from their trick cans but still have one good life-saving pop left. "You could charge a hundred-fifty each, easy. Give me ten bucks and you can give your grandkids a bath toy."

He accepts the seat belts in his warped hands, then gently lays them back in the trunk without touching any part of the car.

"Ten more on the hub assembly," she asks.

Lester shuts the trunk. "I don't open that crypto crap before seven."

4

THE SISTER

SHE SPENDS twenty hours a week in a car, another thirty-ish underneath them, and so every car-free setting is a godsend. Inside RiteAid, she walks down Aisle 12 for no reason other than to streak her hand along the tall sweating coolers. She squeezes the button of a skeleton in the Halloween Aisle. It's not a talker. The red eyes shine until she lets go.

She carries yellow rubber gloves, green Tic-Tacs, and a Twix to the registers. There's an early morning line. A man has a jug of Drano for each hand. A woman's basket contains everything from eyeliner to soup to a bottle of Tylenol as big as a muffler. Pegs scrolls her phone to see if there's been some kind of shortage announced related to any of the woman's purchases. She checks Rūm—no new apartments. The CounterCash has the same script for each customer. Pegs can mumble the basics by the time she's paying: *"Welcome to...scan your...would you like to...all sales before the first surge help Pittsburgh's pet population."*

She opens the Twix in her building's lobby and chews it walking down the stairwell, which hasn't known fresh air in a decade. *Century* might be more accurate. Still, it's a welcome change from aggressive Freon.

Less welcome is the sight of shiny jewel-like mice shit in the basement hallway. She spots the furry jewelers themselves in separate traps, squeakless, super dead. She kicks one trap to the other. The devices were too distant for one death to properly warn the other, though maybe it wouldn't have mattered. She bundles the traps in her sturdy spandex-like Revo rain jacket, shoulders through the door to the communal laundry, and opens her coat above the trash. She adds the Twix wrapper as an attempt to hide the mice. It winds up looking like a space blanket on the smaller one.

She holds the coat away from herself the rest of the way down the hall. She uses two fingers to extract her keys and dumps the jacket beside her sister's on the tarp in the living room. She pairs the Tic-Tacs and the yellow gloves on the kitchen counter. "We need traps," she tells her sister.

"The icemaker is pooling." Avery flips her omelet, points the spatula at the fridge. A small pool of water sits on two puckered tiles.

"Did you look at it?"

"Sticking body parts into machines is your department."

"I've got to eat, then drive." Pegs sits with Fruit Loops, milk, coffee. "I'm seven short on the road."

"How short on sleep?"

"Driving pays."

Avery keeps pinching and tearing omelet, eating straight from the pan. The girl can't feel heat—years of handling espresso for men who wear soft waterproof shoes and women who write poems and emails about rain. Pegs has driven past the cafe on so many test routes that she has come to associate the front square window with Avery's face. Both are minimalist in decor. There's no advertisements or flash—what's the point with surges coming? Both Avery and the shop window look bright, spotless, quietly fashionable. Both trade in hot bitterness that won't think twice about burning the overeager. Avery instructs Pegs to sleep, it's not healthy, particularly given how much she drives and uses her phone while doing so. Avery's warning: I don't want you waking up in a river.

"Our Rūm account renewed itself." Pegs chews, twists her cereal. "Such a racket. There was nothing new."

Raindrops plink the high glass block. It's not enough rain to create a river along the sidewalk. Pegs stands, stepping over the fridge leak, which she could swear is already sniffing a new tile. She raises her fingers to where the window becomes wall. "Caulk is only going to do so much," she says.

Avery points up at the window. "You'll need to do to the plywood and tires, out on the sidewalk. It worked last year."

"Something will pop for November first."

"The wind woke me." Avery's mouth steams with egg. She slips into the rubber gloves and rinses forks and glasses. "I expected a shelter alert."

The phrase *shelter alert* sends a shiver through Pegs. More specifically, it shoots a flutter to her hip. She touches her empty pocket, though her phone is on the table. She cannot yet deal with shelter alerts. They wreck a day. They trigger every phone like some kind of hellish communal alarm clock, forcing everyone to awaken to a new reality—whatever you're doing no longer matters, get home, stay there. Sometimes shelter alerts provide thirty minutes notice. Sometimes it's a full day. The alerts cause traffic jams, then empty roads. They cause entire classes of workers, like Avery, to forfeit paychecks. This year they will also cause a microscopically small group of workers to take driverless cars out into surges to see if the upgrades are worth the trouble. "We've got time before the first alert," Pegs says.

Avery turns off the water and says: we better. She says she's banking on at least a month more of shifts. She can't afford a full November stuck on surge pay. She definitely can't in some higher, pricier apartment. "If we lose an income," she says, "we're going to be at Mom and Dad's by Christmas."

"Why? My room is even lower there."

"Not the living room." Avery removes her gloves and hangs them in a frown over the split in the sinks. Pegs watches them until they fall. It's maddening. The insides get wet. Pegs voices this. She says can they *please* have one dry thing. She says she doesn't want mold in new gloves. Avery points at the fridge, the puddle, you first.

"I'm behind," Pegs says.

"It's only Wednesday. Sleep."

"I'm finding us an apartment. Today. On my drive."

"If something happens to you, we're screwed."

"Nothing ever happens."

"You're a walking Disattentive."

Pegs tells her little sister it's *Inattentive*, that the cars prevent anything truly horrible from taking place, that Revo can't just jettison their test drivers. Revo is desperate. The clock is ticking. They're on their last business pivot before they pivot to drones or trucking or nonexistence.

Avery slides open the door to their shallow pantry. Four jugs of blue wiper fluid are stacked atop a box of GripRite gloves that may or may not be from Revo. Slowly, glacially, the Coffee Cone rolls out. It navigates as though the brewing mechanism in its chest has shot coffee into the nine cups on its top tray, though the nine cups are empty, the spouts above them dry. The Cone's blue eyes blink. All told, the Coffee Cone's eyes, height, and stoutness aren't much different from the red-eyed skeleton in RiteAid. It's unclear why the company who makes the automated rolly things thought a brown upside-down traffic cone was the most enticing design. It's possible they want vaguely to

associate their coffee with an enema, in which case—sure. The
Cone is less than graceful as it rolls over a tear in the linoleum.

"What about her?" Avery says. "Would they cut you loose for
this?"

The Cone rolls to the fridge. It stops an inch from the water.
It sniffs. "That cone," says Pegs, "is worth two grand."

"We don't need it."

"I need coffee when you're not around," Pegs says. The cone
reroutes. It passes her chair. It rolls to the tarp of rain jackets,
sniffs, reroutes.

Avery lifts her jacket and suits up. She tells Pegs to stuff the
coffee cone in the pantry.

"You freed it," Pegs says.

"You stole it."

"Two grand!"

"So pawn it already." Avery shakes Tic-Tacs straight into her
mouth and zips her jacket. "Better yet, fix the fridge, then get
some sleep. I'll text if there's new apartments."

5

LION TAMING IN
OUTER SPACE

PEGS LOOKS at her mattress on the floor, but doesn't lower herself to it. She doesn't jam her head inside their freezer to search for the icemaker leak, either.

She unlocks her phone. She paces the kitchen, authenticating her identity in LedgerCoin. Out of Lester's fifty bucks for the hub assembly, she divvies $16.68 to herself. She drinks coffee twice before sending $16.66 to Leah and Anna. She exercises every pipe in the bathroom and then buckles herself behind the wheel of BlueGill3 and begins the mandatory cool down. The AC goosepimples her exposed neck. Her short wet hair turns to icicles. She swears she can feel Freon squirming in her throat.

Onscreen, she calls up Wednesday's itinerary. Revo has assigned her fifteen destinations, with ten additional suggestions in the event she finishes her test routes early. Some of the destinations have been flagged for a new route development, some she has traveled over twenty times, and none of them scream *apartments*. None are near neighborhoods dotted with tall apartment buildings because buildings like that don't really exist in Pittsburgh. It's as though the city stopped building housing when it stopped making steel. The most readily available high options tend to be the second and third floors of houses,

which people rent out for prices that read more like tuition. This
will almost surely be the case in Friendship, where there's some
new traffic circle that needs to be navigated. The new bus stop
in the Hill District is high up, and the Black neighborhoods are
cheap, but they get zero in the way of drainage infrastructure, so
it's a wash in every sense.

She considers checking Rūm but immediately zips her phone
inside her jacket. One more Inattentive means a retrain. A retrain means an unpaid hour, possibly two. No thanks.

She drives ten minutes without an Inattentive, then ten more.
She scans the real world for real apartment ads. She has already
seen both the real and digital versions of every possible living
space. She anticipates the second-floor advertisement on Liberty Avenue. She doesn't need to look it up—it's for November
second, and it's for $3,700 a month. She knows the green build-
ing on Bryant Street in Highland Park keeps all its rental signs
high and that the availabilities are all on the first floor.

The car parks at its Presbyterian destination. She punches in
a new target. It's an easy route, save the rush hour aspect, which
is extending past nine. Pittsburghers are out. They can feel those
surges coming. They're mobile while it's advisable. She swears
some cars, like her own, don't have actual destinations. She loops
downtown behind a Taurus looking for some magical parking
space, a spot that was open every single time in the 2020s when
the driver was younger and available asphalt was a given. In the
end it seems like the Taurus is just trying to catch a glimpse of
the old-timey movie production frantically trying to finish its
shoot by the courthouse before the crank-started cars overheat
or explode. Two straight businesses are boarding windows. A
flatbed delivering plywood is half on a downtown sidewalk, half
on the street. Nobody has a problem with this.

Nobody human, that is. BlueGill3 waits behind the flatbed.

There's an obvious moment where the prototype could circle the truck before the next rush of cars through the emerging mist, but BG3 opts for patience. It doesn't trust humans.

The wood delivery guy, on the other hand, is trusting and then some. He jumps on and off the flatbed without looking at the street, the sidewalk, the low school of drones, anywhere. The guy is about to make more money in October 2030 than in the year's first nine months combined. He's working like he knows it. The flatbed is full. The plywood is bound together with huge thick black straps. The delivery guy rips a knife through the binding and lifts the top piece off the stack so it can go take its beating.

Stiff back in Manchester. Cat living in a dry cube under a dripping mailbox in the Mexican War Streets. The sun appears briefly above the baseball stadium and then sinks as newer, fuller clouds float her way, carrying storms in their guts. The salon where she got a breakup chop a million years ago, right before driving got added to her plate? Packed. It's like people don't work. It's like people expect their hair to grow three times faster once surges hit. There's a rent sign in the next block. Like all the other signs, it's posted on the second floor. Unlike the others signs, this one isn't familiar. She hasn't seen it in real life or phone life. She can't quite tell whether she's in Fineview or the Northside. It's possible that Fineview and the Northside are the same thing. She's past the building before she can memorize the number.

She touches the console screen, reroutes. It's a bit early to hit the McDonald's by the stadiums for her pee allowance, but apartments: they go fast. Second floors live for an hour online, sometimes minutes. A minute on her phone in McDonald's is all she needs.

Construction slows her near the National Aviary. Four guys in hard hats aren't doing much of anything. They're looking

up at the condors in their outdoor cages, maybe betting on
which would survive if the birds got left out in a surge. Her
tires advance two, maybe three full rotations. The cars ahead of
her sneak through the available gap. She stares into the horn.
Honk, she thinks. *Do something!* Little happens. The steering
wheel moves without her input, jiggering and bobbing with
the random pointlessness of a newborn. She pictures other
desperate people seeing the ad, calling the number, signing a
lease.

Pegs coughs. It's a theatrical cough. She lunges forward. She
unzips her pocket. She doesn't extract tissue or a handkerchief.
She unlocks her phone. She keeps her hand in her pocket. She
stares straight through the windshield. She rolls past the condors and workers. Slowly, blindly, she touches the apartment
app. The BlueGill is aping her deliberate pace. It's moving so
freaking slow. The cars lined up for breakfast at the drive-thru
wrap around the brick building, and the BlueGill treats this
laneless traffic like a jungle rope bridge missing every other goddamn plank. BG3 won't budge. It purrs in place. Two parking
spots are open, but now families are exiting the building on foot.
A Volvo with a dangling exhaust is reversing. She debates disabling the system, parking, calling the apartment listing. She'd
have to answer for disabling. She could possibly argue her way
out of a retrain.

The BlueGill accelerates. Accelerates is strong. It rolls. The
prototype turns into a spot between an F-150 full of plywood
and a Camry. She powers off the system. She rips her phone
from her pocket. The apartment app is distorted. At first, she
thinks it's because she had tried to delete it. Multiple angry
messages clutter the screen. But the messages are not app related. They aren't even apartment related. The messages are not
her sister saying, *OMG affordable high one, if you would just sell off
the stupid coffee cone we'll have first and last.* The messages aren't

Revo HQ saying, *We think it's just so great you pulled over rather than attempting to search for that apartment while driving.* The incoming messages are from the other test drivers.

LEAH: *$16.66 is so disrespectful*

ANNA: *I ran an analysis of four online retailers and at bare...*

Leah does not address a single item from Anna's long text. Instead:

LEAH: *WE. NEED. A. WHOLE. CAR.*

This is Leah's whole thing: more. Whereas Pegs merely wants more feet and inches between her and the ground, Leah wants more space for everyone. Whereas Pegs wants some tangible cash, Leah wants to wield nine kinds of intangible power over Revo and society and probably some uncle that was mean to her once. Pegs wants to skim some parts on the sly. Leah wants to shove all two hundred Revo employees into a driverless prototype, lock the doors, and then sell it to some art gallery for a million a head so they can hang the car as an example of clima-techno-capital something or other, all without ever once whispering the word: *risk*.

Pegs swipes away the texts. She finds the nearby apartment in Rūm, calls the number. She tells the woman she saw the sign, the one in Fineview, or the Northside, the brown one.

"We've got two left," the woman tells her.

"How high up?"

Men return to their truck of plywood. One guy gets in and hangs his arm out the window like a St. Bernard's tongue on a summer day. It's like he expects Pegs to grab on.

"I'm down the block," Pegs says.

"One is November first, the other is the fifteenth," the woman says. "Every window has been reinforced."

"What floor?"

"Once you're a tenant," the woman says, "you get bidding rights whenever there's openings. So, next year..."

When the woman finishes her pitch, Pegs goes into McDonald's and pees. It's not enough to have warranted the early stop. She loiters on the dry tile, a few paces behind the line. The pros of a Coke: she could use the company. The cons: it's an expenditure. Plus, she has just now used a pee before noon.

She engages the BlueGill's system, Coke-less. She departs the lot onto Allegheny Ave, which is shaded by delivery drones. They fly in pairs, ten or so feet above the telephone wires. There's enough pairs for the street to feel like a tunnel. She can't see the beginning of the long flying line. The Toyota Tacoma ahead of her tries to find it. The truck speeds through the red light that the BlueGill stops at. Pegs wonders if the driver was arrogant or in a hurry. It's possible the driver just got caught watching the delivery drones. They have to fly the same speed limit as the cars so as not to throw off drivers' sense of speed, but the problem is that the drones monkey with other perceptions, too. When the caboose of the airborne fleet passes overhead, Pegs can feel it in her foot—the impulse to catch it. She counsels herself to ignore this impulse. She tries to relax, to burrow inside the day, to just…be. She tells herself to ignore the next line of delivery drones. She does not look at a single window in the next apartment building she passes. It's dangerous to hunt for apartments while test driving. It is most definitely lunacy to turn pee breaks into massive inner struggles about whether to buy a Coke. The whole apartment thing pressurizes her. She tells herself to simply act like everything else—a brainless entity ferried along by automation.

It's not a relaxing thought. She often has the thought that she's becoming a package. She is constantly transported yet entirely still. Her life is full of motionless motion.

She reminds herself that she's a human. On the Tenth Street Bridge, she thinks of herself as a vehicular lion tamer.

Actually it's more like a security guard, glued to a monitor.

Physically, she's trapped in what her mother would call a loony bin. There's pads on the door and dash. The inflatable seat belt is ready to fire up a straight jacket at any moment.

She decides she is a lonely astronaut floating through space, except she is doing so on Earth, inside a clearly defined geofence. She orbits through one hundred thirty-three hilly neighborhoods, where the buildings get drabber the higher the Blue-Gill climbs. More likely, it's that the materials get cheaper, i.e. there's not much in the way of high-altitude brick and stone, except then, all of a sudden, the apex up on Mount Washington becomes a god's canvas—glass, three car garages, new paint jobs every spring after the surges blast off last year's color. The church is readying to become a shelter. Bins are out for canned goods. A guy with a high-quality butt is on a ladder fretting over stained glass. She wonders if ladder man will be staying in the shelter. She wonders if she could volunteer. Or live there. Or volunteer and live there. It'd be a bit of a hike for her to get down to Revo. Downtown is so far below the road. She can see the bridges but not the drainage holes polka-dotting their sides. It's insane how far away it all looks.

It's even more insane that a deer made it up onto Mount Washington. She idles beside the dead clump at a red light. The wet doe is pushed to the curb. Rain leaks off its airless nose like drip coffee, and that rubbery nose may as well be an arrow, because on a dead line, up the street, Pegs sees it: an apartment. The second floor sign actually says: *Live Right Here.* There are no visible objects or clutter in the room. The place looks ready. The motionless fan is like a quiet drone from a more peaceful century. She's sure it's too expensive. Second floor? On Mount Washington? Forget it.

But: the sign looks raggedy. Raggedy is preferable. Raggedy

is affordable. The cross-traffic still has a green light. An Escalade tails a Kia Soul. Pegs coughs into her left hand. Her right covers her phone in her pocket. She slides it to her lap. She can see the phone number clearly on the second-floor sign. She dials blindly, her eyes drilling tunnels through the windshield. She won't call the number. Not yet. She'll simply have it ready. There's a Subway she can stop at. Avery worked there, a million years ago. Cross traffic is still moving. The light turns yellow. A white truck sneaks through. She drops her eyes to double-check the number. She can't see it through all the texts.

LEAH, TO PEGS AND ANNA: *I unloaded on Lester*

LESTER, TO PEGS: *New rule—you're the only one allowed in*

AVERY: *check this apt!!! Ill call it wen slow*

It's a link to an apartment. The apartment is the one on Mount Washington, the one that's half a block away from the red light. Pegs clicks the listing. It's a bit steep—$2500 per month. But: it's a legitimate second floor. The biggest window is the only impact window, but the installation looks new, or at least newish. She and Avery would be closer to their parents, further from work. Avery couldn't walk. There's always their father's car. The logistics? Hell. Hell and then some. The prototypes are of no use. No untrained passengers are allowed in a driverless prototype like BlueGill3, which rolls into the intersection then jolts to a stop. The seat belt bites her chest. The car behind her honks. The screen beeps. The words are red.

DISENGAGED—INATTENTIVE.

6

THE PROTESTER

THE INATTENTIVE ALERT doesn't remain on screen very long. Pegs taps *Yes* once, *No* once. She switches the BlueGill to manual and gasses through the intersection. She drives to the stone apartment building. The folding chair blocking the long parking space is no obstacle, not today. She rams it with such conviction and at such an angle that the chair winds up on the wet sidewalk. She parks. She calls the number on her phone. It matches the one on the sign above her, the one that says *Live Right Here*. She debates knocking on the front door. The number rings.

BlueGill3 starts ringing, too. The car is off, but the console screen is lighting up.

Incoming: Revo HQ

Janice Pegula: Accept?

Between rental rings, she touches *Accept*. She tells the car: "Just a drone scare, all good."

"Calling all cars." It's a man. Worse, it's Yabner. He's an engineer of some kind in his forties who desperately wants to be in his twenties. She can hear his hair dye through the speakers. The stuff makes his hair look orangey. He thinks it comes out blonde. He also thinks safety shifts are so far beneath him. You'd think he was the only employee put in a pinch when the company shrank from six hundred to three hundred. "If you're scrolling and you know it, come on home." He claps. Or clucks.

"I wasn't."

"We could screen the footage," Yabner says. "Sell tickets."

"Two more hours."

"You're maxed on Inattents." No one calls them this. "That's a re-train, coming down the tracks."

In her ear, the ringing stops. A woman speaks on Pegs' cell. "Shuler Realty, this is Amy."

"Hi just....hang..." Pegs mutes herself. She leans forward. The car's mic is somewhere in the rear view mirror. She whispers, to Yabner: "Free oil change." She adds: "And a tire rotation. I need two hours."

"God bless the greasy soul whose best bribe is an oil change. Christ."

"For a year," she adds. "Two."

"I bike," Yabner tells her. "Or shuttle. I sold the Mustang."

The bright Amy The Realtor person: "Are you calling about a property in Oakland, Polish Hill—"

Yabner's voice is loud through the speakers. "What did you just call me?"

Pegs unmutes her phone. She tells the realtor the address of the property in question, Mount Washington, the stone one, just wait one moment while I bring my drone delivery inside. Pegs mutes her phone, covers it. She asks Yabner for two more driving hours. She says she'll come in after, she swears. She needs to hit seven hours today to make quota.

"It's Wednesday," Yabner says. "Re-train tonight, drive tomorrow."

"Re-trains are unpaid."

"Here at Revo, safety is one of the four pillars in our logo, upholding—"

Yabner is drowned out by a honk. The honk is on Pegs' end, not his. It's right behind her. The second honk lasts even longer. The BlueGill's trunk is in the street, catching rain meant for the asphalt. It's blocking traffic, evidently. A U-Haul fills the tiny rear windshield.

Pegs starts the car. The call with Yabner evaporates. She drives the BlueGill more fully into the long parking spot and puts the phone on speaker. She tells the realtor she can look at the second-floor apartment, right now.

"That listing is unfortunately gone."

"I can see the sign." Pegs looks at her phone, the listing. It was posted within the hour.

"It's that time of year," says Amy Shuler.

"I'm outside." True. "I could give you a full year, cash, at the door." Not true. The honking intensifies. Pegs takes herself off speaker. She cups her hand over her phone and mouth. She says nothing.

"The two available are lower," the woman tells her. "November first."

"Is the contract signed? For the upstairs."

"Once you're in the building," Amy tells her, "you get bidding rights on higher listings."

Someone approaches the car. The person is carrying a chair. It happens to be the same folding chair that Pegs politely guided to the sidewalk. The man holding it is from the U-Haul. He says nothing. He simply holds the chair in front of himself as calmly as an ID in a prison photo or the pitchfork in *American Gothic*. It's as though Pegs has violated some sacred contract, though this is not what Pegs wants to discuss with him. She wants to roll down the window and ask: How did you get an apartment? She wants to know if he's moving into the unit on the second floor, the one with the sign, posted an hour ago. It's possible he's

moving into a different room. Probable, actually. Still, she wants
to ask if he shells out for premium levels of apartment apps or
just slums it, does he work, is apartment hunting his full-time
job, what's his secret, then the screen lights up. *Incoming: Revo.*
It's Yabner. No debate, he says. She needs to come in, now. She
needs to schedule her retrain, and no, he isn't sticking around to
do it. He's done.

So is Pegs. She quits on the day, fully. She flat out shuts down
on the route to Revo. She allows herself to feel numb. It's better
than stewing about a retrain, how it will cost her money, how
she'll have to make up for it with more stolen parts, and she tells
herself again: Just numb out, dude. She tells her body to sleep
with her eyes open.

She focuses on her breathing. She exhales all throughout
downtown, beneath the Amtrak, into the commerce of the
river-hugging Strip District, where all of the AV companies
reside. Driverless prototypes abound. They prance through the
Strip District like showhorses before an unregulated cash race.
At the first stop sign on Smallman Street, Pegs stops behind a
Norroyo. It's mayo white, compact, big on cameras. Lenses are
everywhere. They're rowed above each headlight and taillight. It's
like someone snuck four Goodyear's into a time machine, then
a mall, then welded the tires onto a Sunglasses Hut kiosk. She's
heard the test drivers at Norroyo are responsible for polishing
each camera lens. They supposedly use some kind of special rag
and solution, the Cinderellas of the Driverless Sunglasses Hut.

On the next block she can feel the nineteenth century rum-
bling the tires as she is driven 25.99 mph alongside a six-wheeler from Ryde. The extra wheels represent the company's "surge
pivot." The whole design makes little sense. The Ryde prototypes
look more likely to clamber over the sandbags into the Allegheny than to serve any protective purpose whatsoever against

surges that spit benches, trash cans, and drones into vehicles. The Ryde driver does not strike Pegs as more relaxed thanks to two extra Coopers. The woman seems tense. Pegs wishes she could see the woman's teeth. She's heard Ryde offers its contract workers healthcare after six months. It's possible this is a rumor. It's possible that the offer does not include dental. None of it is worth getting too excited over, seeing as the AV sector's non-compete agreements basically ensure that wherever you start your AV career is where it will end. How you're treated is private and final.

The protesters offer a refreshing contrast in that their disdain for test drivers is quite public. The Ryde prototype beats Pegs to the gathering at Smallman and 21st. There's a dozen protesters this evening, ish. They hold their cardboard signs against the wind. The slogans have barely survived a day of rain. Sharpie oozes:

Surge Pay Expansion NOW!
S.P.E. for ALL
Safe. Practical. Ethical.

Not every sign is related to surge pay. There's some climate and carbon stuff. One sign is about how climate fear shouldn't mean we just give ourselves over to automation. The slogan is too wordy to be memorably effective. At least two protesters are in masks—a tonguey zombie and some kind of butchered bull's head. The masks freak her out. *Chill her willikens*, as her dad would say. The two nuns in habit are paired like batteries. The nuns are for some reason scarier than the folks in masks. It's scarier because the nuns are not masquerading. They're real.

The Ryde prototype in front of Pegs stops. Rather: the six-wheel Ryde car gets snared in a trap. The nuns have extended traffic objects into the street. They stand in front of the Ryde prototype waving an orange traffic cone and a yield sign. It's like they're advertising a car wash for dump trucks. Meanwhile, the other protesters scatter amongst the stalled traffic. They extend S.P.E leaflets to car windows. Drivers who refuse them get leaflets pinned to their windshield.

The nuns hold strong as the human drivers beep and curse. A protestor in a soggy jean jacket approaches Pegs' window. He's got work boots, a mustache. He seems like the kind of guy who wouldn't care one bit about the effect of AVs on labor, privacy, the environment, anything. He's a guy that probably doesn't trust AVs because he just wants to drive an American car himself. His surly approach to the BlueGill indicates that, in his mind, autonomous vehicles may as well stand for Asshole Volvo-owners.

The man is directed toward another car by the head protester. She's in a skeleton mask. Her blonde hair spills out of what looks to be thick, hot rubber. The mask's bony expression is a smile, like the skeleton just died, peacefully. The skeleton steps to Pegs' window with a kind of bowlegged athleticism. Its tall galoshes are blinking-lights-on-a-cell-tower red, and while Pegs hates how much attention Leah draws to herself, she's at least grateful Leah isn't wearing her Revo-issued jacket out in public at a rainy protest.

Pegs switches to manual. She lowers the window. "I just got hit with a retrain."

Leah runs a finger along the roof. She finishes at the windshield. It isn't clear whether she's speaking through the skeleton's nose or mouth: "Be a shame if this car just disappeared, Miss."

"In broad daylight? Twenty witnesses?"

"I slide in, we drive this here nice BlueGill to Lester's, take it apart piece by—"

"You wouldn't know which wheel goes first."

"Thus the Pegs."

Pegs hates what Leah does to her name. *The Pegs. Pegula-*

Rula. Pegster. The worst: *Peggy.* She knows Leah is making some proud bedeviled face inside the mask, though it's impossible to tell. The mask is creepy. It's even creepier when the soundtrack is thunder. The full-on storm sounds three neighborhoods away, unlike all the honking, which is aggressive and quite present. It feels like shoving. Traffic begins to pass on Pegs' left. Leah extends her metal stop sign toward the cars. The drivers do not obey it. Leah keeps the sign raised, a swatter awaiting a fly. She doesn't even need to swing when the white Norroyo approaches. Its cameras spot the sign, and it slows. The Norroyo stops itself ten full feet from Leah. The test driver is unfazed. She disengages the system, unlocks her phone.

"See that zombie?" Leah points at a protester in a one-eyed zombie mask. The thing has gums for days. "She drives for Ryde."

"In that?"

"I was thinking we stage a carjacking of them, they do us, then we wind up with two full cars and their parts."

Pegs waves off a guy trying to hand her a leaflet. "We need less people, not more."

"What we need," Leah says, "is to leverage our pathetic invisibility within our industry to gut every—"

"I can barely hear you."

Leah lifts her rubber bones. Her cheeks are red, blotched. She breathes real air. She transfers the stop sign in her hands. Her blue eyes acclimate. They grow. They're insistent. Leah's eyes are always so...forward. They're like the tetras or bettas Avery kept plopping into that dumb filterless bowl as a kid, the headstrong ones that kept darting at the glass like there was liberation or rapture or the most handsomest fish ever just a quick hard swim away. Leah tambourines the stop sign with each word. "We. Need. A. Car."

"You don't think they'll notice if a fish leaves the tank?"

"Ten bucks a hub cap isn't cutting it."

Pegs doesn't say that they were hub *assemblies*. She doesn't remind Leah that they're splitting the profit three ways. Four, if you factor Lester. Pegs checks the rearview. She can't see past the third car. One guy opens his door. He doesn't get out. Pegs tries to appease Leah, telling her there's more money coming their way. She explains that Lester took every new item except the seat belts.

"I gave him nothing." Leah spits. The skeleton mask falls. It covers her eyes. She lifts it. "Showed him the trunk and pulled right back out."

Pegs scratches her knees. She breathes. She tells herself not to say *I*. *I* doesn't play with Leah. "We need every penny."

"There's got to be other buyers."

Pegs grabs the bottom of the open window with both hands. Her head departs the car. "There are ten thousand dead machines for every Lester that wants them. Ten million."

"You have to be willing to walk away."

Leah wipes sweat and rain from her forehead. She holds the stop sign in front of the Norroyo with both hands. Pegs wads up her gloveless hands near her mouth. She screams vowels into them. She starts near *E*, ends near *A*. She tells Leah that she's behind on hours. She needs a retrain. Every affordable apartment in the worthless city is in the goddamn basement at the bottom of some hill. She doesn't need Leah proving points.

Pegs breathes. "Did anyone see you unloading the parts back at Revo?"

Leah points down 21st street, toward the river. "They're chilling."

A block down, Pegs can see it: a RedGill straddling the sidewalk. The angle of the tilt is severe. The lidar and its helmet on top are like a wedding cake about to topple. She envisions the parts leaning left in the trunk, mashing each other, breaking.

"You parked?" Pegs says. "Here? With a full trunk?"

The shorter nun sees Pegs mimicking Leah's point. The woman interprets it as some sort of alliance. She gives Pegs a very intense, very Romanesqe thumbs up. She's like a soggy little emperor that survived a drowning in whatever river the Romans drank from.

Leah hides her face in the mask. She says the RedGill is locked.

"They lock themselves." Pegs stops scratching her knees. She counsels herself: *Speak normal. Calm.* "Anyone cutting out early from Revo is going to spot it."

The skeleton scoffs. Leah says they all bike the river trails to their lofts. Or shuttle.

"You're taking too many risks," Pegs says.

"You're the one that needs a retrain, Pegsy."

Pegsy: a true sin. And then some. Leah knows this. She pays for it by having to deal with the male driver who finally departs through his open car door. He yells at Leah—*Hey Bones, yeah you, we have lives, quit your bitching, get off the street, get a job.* Leah interrupts with—*Better surge pay keeps people safe, it keeps people home, the driverless car companies would just love you, they're banking on you needing to go to work in a surge instead of staying home, safe and paid.* All the back and forth alerts the owner of the donut joint. The guy exits his store. He waves his arms low like the river has overflowed and left fish and plastics all over his walk. He says he's calling the cops. They better have a permit.

Leah lowers the stop sign. She releases the Norroyo upstream. The yeller returns to his idling car. The protesters march off toward some new spot in the AV salmon run. Leah doesn't follow, not immediately. She chucks a leaflet inside Pegs' BlueGill like a Frisbee full of words. Leah adds a few more herself: "Save me a coffee in the garage."

7

KNOCK KNOCK

WHEN IT comes to being perpetually short on their road hours, Pegs and Leah have their reasons. Some are even semi-legitimate, i.e. non-theft-related.

Pegs has her maintenance shifts to blame.

Leah has a brutal commute to Revo from her parents'. Plus: protesting.

But Anna: Anna is never behind on her road hours. Anna never wastes a single moment of a single rainy October day. Not Anna, who wears those ducky toes-out water shoes. Not Anna, who always loads the heaviest parts in the left side of the trunk so as to minimize oscillation on the very right-turn-heavy route to Lester's.

Anna, who went to school for technical robot stuff.

Anna, who actually believes in AV and has definitely told strangers that autonomous vehicles will reduce auto deaths and traffic and the fat content of the mac and cheese at every fish fry in Allegheny County.

AV Anna, who thought test driving would give her a foothold in the industry.

AV Anna, who has been so radically disabused of this notion that she turned AV-positive to AV-negative faster than an inflatable seat belt popping into action.

Anna, who is still able to keep "AV as an idea" and "AV as an employer" separate in her head in a way Pegs and Leah flat-out cannot. Anna has at times said that AV will do no less than expand the mobility horizon. She really uses words like *mobility horizon*. Mobility horizon!

But Anna is not interested in discussing mobility horizons when she approaches Pegs in Revo's garage. She's not interested in discussing "AV as an idea" and "AV as an employer." She zig-zags with righteous purpose through the prototypes. Pegs quickly busies herself at one of the roving computer stations. The stand-up wheely desk contraptions are a bit like a dental hygienist's cart, only the drills and saliva suckers are replaced with wires and screens, and Pegs finds herself wishing she had some kind of oral instrument she could jab in Anna's mouth before it starts unloading gripes. Pegs unholsters the charging hose from the cart, and before she can even insert it into BlueGill3, Anna is on her. She wants to know why she's risking her entire graduate degree and adult career path for $16.66 in LedgerCoin. Lester, she says, is short-changing them. She's got proof. Numbers, stats, and arguments explode out of her open gray Revo rain jacket. She says she cross-referenced prices from multiple suppliers. The median—

Pegs stuffs Leah's surge-pay leaflet to the bottom of a trash can. She opens the BlueGill's trunk. She removes the seat belts that Lester didn't want, then scans the fleet from the rear. There's eleven prototypes in the garage—four BlueGills in the back row, four GreenGills in the middle, and, what with Leah still out in her fully-loaded godforsaken RedGill, only three Reddies up front. The average passerby would think all the gray prototypes are identical minus the colored slashes on the doors; this average person would not spend twenty hours a week driving them, nor another thirty rectifying every cosmetic blemish; they wouldn't fully grasp that every car is both a singular form of an emerging technology and an advertisement for said technology. The ceiling lights in the two-story garage are both very high and incredibly powerful, and they reveal every imperfection. A lidar helmet on a BlueGill looks... foggy. Pegs has no idea why GreenGill3 makes a bigger mess than all the other cars, but there GG3 is, parked in a puddle in the middle row. A tire on RedGill2 looks just the slightest touch low. None of these conditions are a crisis, except the marketing lady is always demanding photos, every other freaking day. The woman expects the garage to look like a high-end car dealership on Pluto, i.e. can you please remove the spills and hide those open Igloo coolers filled with tools that look like weapons? It's a lot of cleanliness to ask of a space that's as big as a high school gymnasium. More specifically, the garage with its residual rain and oils is like a gym after a big game against a rival, when every concession-stuffed attendee is exiting and the janitors are having a pre-mop smoke and every square inch is glistening with both clear liquids and bubbly dark ones.

Cleaning occupies a truly dumb amount of Pegs' garage hours. In part this is because there's rarely anything majorly, truly wrong with the vehicles. Seeing as the company is down to three test drivers in its post-pivot existence, the actual mileage put on any one of the twelve prototypes is minimal. It's not like there's a busted tranny one night and a re-wire the next. Many nights, Pegs' garage hours mostly entail de-smudging lidar helmets and making sure drivers have enough charge in whatever vehicle they'll be driving next.

Anna, meanwhile, is fully charged. And then some.

"I've charted it, and we need to make smarter sales," she says. "Lester takes twice as long to move electrical parts as chassis."

"Does the tire on that RedGill look low?"

"I've got loans, Pegs."

Pegs zags through the BlueGills. There's no scrapes, no pearly windshield dents. She veers toward the mobile coffee cone. There's a single cup on the top tray. She will not save it for Leah. To hell with Leah. To hell and then some. She removes the heating stick, presses the injector. It's out of milk. The side compartment is full of wrappers, not creamer. Holstered waters form a ribcage.

"When I started," Pegs says, "there were scones. Every morning."

Anna waits for Pegs to straighten. She looks at her, eye to eye. Anna tells Pegs that she's been texting, with Leah. She knows Leah drove off without delivering parts to Lester. Anna thinks it's a good idea. They need to be bolder. Next time I go, Anna says, I'm bringing data. Lester is going to pay them whatever the group decides, in advance.

"It's all fluid." Pegs sips. The coffee is blistering without cream. She runs a finger across a clear lidar helmet. She sniffs it.

"It's flowing badly." Anna recreates each bad component of what she deems to be a deteriorating process—the slow payments, the low payments, the risks to their employment, the lack of time left before surges hit and they can't load parts because the garage is full of men. The girl uses too many words in her sentences. The weird thing about it is that she uses all these words while keeping her face as stoic as a historic plaque. Pegs tries to ooze away with the two seat belts and coffee. Anna tails her to the supply room. She's a coffee cone with legs.

"We need bigger payouts," Anna says.

"Jack a Norroyo," Pegs says, "with Leah. See how long before some cop is ringing your apartment."

Pegs hangs her rain jacket on a hook. She turns, slightly, barely, to gauge how the line landed. Anna's shoulders have collapsed like a cheap umbrella. She scares so easily.

"We at least need to escalate how much we deliver," Anna says. "Fast. Before surges."

"I've got a whole system for what goes and when." Pegs doesn't. Her system is about as organized as the supply room, which is the type of cluttered place where a person might think to crank open a window and shoot a president, though, like everywhere else in the garage, it's windowless. There's so many parts and boxes leftover from when the fleet ran fifty deep. The free-standing plastic shelving units make the room seem as though a floundering AutoZone had a lovechild with a crypt. Empty boxes from the caf are stuffed here and there to make the room appear less stolen-from. If you look closely, which no one ever does, you can see that coolant touches vacant kale.

Pegs chucks the seat belts onto a high shelf. She straps on goggles. She shakes two glass cleaners and takes the emptier one to the fleet.

"Say they let us go tomorrow," Anna says. "We've just forfeited all the profit sitting in that room."

"They need us for surge season."

"The only thing this company has ever proved is that it has no idea what anybody needs."

Pegs steps onto a stool. She sets her coffee on the hood and sprays a Venn Diagram on BlueGill2's clear roof-secured helmet. The rag sheds. Pegs asks Anna to bring a new one from the supply room. Anna returns with a rag and one of the modular electric car batteries that Revo briefly tried during some ill-fated pivot. Anna tries to carry two more batteries on her own. Her legs bend into a first-grader's wobbly O.

Pegs meets her halfway with a dolly. Anna always forgets to use one. She is the type of person who spends so much time thinking about the wheeled inventions of the future that she overlooks those of the past. Revo is full of these folks. Pegs has long suspected that many of her co-workers actually hate the physical entities known as cars. Yabner and Boltz definitely do. They are accustomed to software-related creations that can be replicated ten million times in a millisecond. Yabs and Boltz can slap whatever program or code they write on a shared drive and receive applause or even money from all over the globe.

But cars: cars cannot go profitably viral. Cars cannot be transported easily around the globe. Their parts cannot be texted to Lester or across Revo's garage. The battery Pegs carries is like a small sandbag. It requires both hands.

Anna loads tail and flex pipes onto the dolly and rolls it to the trunk. "We can't fill trunks once surges start," she says, nesting the pipes to the right of the batteries. "Everyone's going to be in the garage, plus what if a breakdown crew shows up to a crash site and the trunk is packed?"

Pegs carries the stool to the puddly GreenGill. She sets the stool on a dryish spot. "We cannot have a committee meeting every time you need to repeat some thought."

Anna is at the GreenGill before Pegs is on the stool. Anna wants to know: what meetings? They never meet. One or two of them reach some random agreement in some random isolated conversation. The decision is randomly communicated to the others, then Lester announces some random price.

"Tell you what." Pegs rags the top of the round helmet. She forgot to spray. She continues ragging. "You go find your own supplier, Leah can take a hot car to hers, then we'll see who does best. I'm happy to cut my costs."

"Identifying inefficiencies is part of a heathy process."

"Feels like whining."

A boom echoes through the garage. The noise is not merely thunder. It suggests an impact. It sounds as though some hard, flat object has struck the exterior of the garage.

Pegs steps off the stool. She leaves one foot high. Anna crouches behind the GreenGill. All four tall garage doors are motionless. None of them rattle or move. The cement is flat.

Anna taps her weather app. "What was it like when you came in?"

"Rainy," Pegs says. "Not a surge, though."

Neither of them has received a shelter alert. Another thudding hard entity smashes a door. Pegs drops her phone. The coffee topples. It rushes down the GreenGill's windshield.

"Call someone," Anna says.

"Which door got hit?"

Pegs leaves her phone on the ground. She raises her goggles. She walks to the front of the gray fleet. The eleven hoods are aimed spear-like at the exits. Rain splatters the four garage doors. She braces for a third boom.

"Dellinger's voicemail," Anna says.

"Call reception."

"That's the other side of the building."

"Keep at Dellinger."

Anna raises her phone. "It was pretty windy this afternoon," she says.

"Not surge-windy." Pegs paces the exits. None of the doors appear damaged. There's no dents. She looks up at the very top of the fourth exit and another boom jolts the whole long garage. The second door gets walloped. It may have been the first. Anna says she wasn't watching.

"It's not even November," Anna says. "It's not a surge."

Pegs isn't so sure. Something is out there. Some as-of-now unnamed force is threatening the doors. In her mind, she sees the river. It sloshes outside the exits. It skips sandbags at Revo. She envisions the wind carrying objects headfirst into the exterior. It throws dumpsters and trash cans. It balls up flocks of birds dumb enough to have stuck around.

Birds don't go boom, though. There's a fourth impact. It's big and…round-sounding, a huge fist. It lands low on door three. The door vibrates. It settles. It's as though someone is testing each door. They're trying to determine which huge sheet of metal is weakest. Then again, she has no idea where the first two booms landed. It could be random.

The first door is struck, and Pegs runs to it. She lowers herself, hands on the cement, and listens for a thud on the asphalt. She hears rain.

"Get away from there," Anna says.

"These doors are a mile." Pegs presses her ear to one. Rain is all she can hear. She thinks she hears wind. It's possibly the ventilation system—whispering, rapping, spitting. Her nerve endings tense. She feels her body glow. Her hairs turn orange and grow their own teeny orange hairs. Her bones can sense another boom, any second. She steps back, hands in front of herself, ready to catch.

Nothing happens. Her orangeness subsides. She tries to watch all four exits at once.

"Still no shelter alert," Anna says. She keeps touching the RedGill at the front of the fleet, like the car is home base in some backyard game.

"How long has it been since the last impact?"

"Should I call 911?"

"Text Dellinger." Pegs turns from the fleet, which seems closer than before. It's like the hoods are inching forward when she isn't looking, squeezing her against the doors, which haven't moved. She touches Door 4. It's cold.

"The text didn't deliver," Anna says.

"Connect to the caf's wireless."

"What's the password this week?"

Pegs eyes shoot left, right, left. They scan slowly left to right. "It's been at least two minutes since the last impact, right?"

"Should I be timing them?"

Pegs walks to the control panel and opens the protection flap. She touches the switch to Door 1.

"You're insane." Anna backtracks around the hood. All ten toes in her stupid shoes are wiggling, tense.

"Whatever hit us is probably just lying there."

"I'm in the menu at reception," Anna says. She presses some number.

"Which door has been hit the least?"

Anna paces. She checks the hallway to the main building. It's empty. She says it makes more sense for Pegs to open the door that has been hit the most. Her thinking is that it's the least likely to get smashed again. Pegs could debate the point, but she wants Anna to feel involved. Plus, she doesn't know shit about probability.

She gets her goggles on. She throws the switch on Door 1.

The door vibrates. Slowly, it begins to rise. The electric hum reverberates. The surge outside is just as loud. Rain hisses at the entranceway. Anna yells words Pegs can't hear over the door and the weather.

Pegs stops the door once it's knee high. She jiggles the switch, coaxing it a bit higher, and stops when the opening is wide enough for her to crawl out. She doesn't exit, though. Not at first. She crouches, head near the floor. Rain splatters her goggles. It soaks the slick interior cement. On all fours, she sneaks herself halfway out.

"In or out," Anna yells. "Don't do *that*."

Pegs' hair is soaked in seconds. Water runs down her neck. It sucks her shirt to her back. The wind tugs her head left. She stares back at it, looking right. It's hard to see much. Rain pounds her goggles as she crabs out further. Her shoulders are drenched, instantly. They become heavy enough to be the booming object that's been smacking the doors.

There's no such object visible. There's no huge rock or sandbag at the bottom of the four exits. Scraps of plywood blow by. There's a dozen, maybe. None are heavy. The rest of the trash is fly-away plastics. They barely hold in place long enough for Pegs to confirm their color.

Puddles form at her hands. It's the water running down her arms. It has more to do with rain assaulting the garage door and then running down thirty feet of metal onto Pegs, but it feels like her arms are sinking. The asphalt is lowering, the water rising. Her palms feel suctioned.

She looks straight out into the storm. She squints and can see the round cement crash poles marking the end of the small paved lot behind Revo. The posts are lined in front of the bike path like a thirty-fingered yellow hand saying: *Stop!* The crash posts aren't there to protect bikers. They're there to protect prototypes from spazzing over the bike path, then the sandbags, then disappearing into the Allegheny River. The trees on the shallow river bank would provide little resistance. The wind bends them violently to the left. It's possible their limbs have been snapping off, blasting the doors.

But there aren't all that many trees. Their parts are thin. And the trees are being blown down river, not at the building. Nothing else is out there. No object is aimed at her. It had to have been something big, she thinks. Only something huge could rattle Revo's doors. It was a massive, pounding force, and whatever it is, it's gone. It's hidden, at any rate.

Then a wooden pallet goes cartwheeling past. A second pallet shatters against a crash post and breaks into three parts, maybe more. A new pallet is blown toward Revo. It veers, aggressively, as though tugged hard by a thick leash, and Pegs is pulled back indoors. The pallet hits Door 3, maybe 4. She doesn't see. Wood scampers past the opening under Door 1. She peeks out. She's pulled in. Rain and fluorescence clog her goggles. A laser is charging. It's the door, lowering.

Dellinger's arm is wet. He is the one who has pulled Pegs back in. His dry arm holds a phone to his ear.

"Leah wrecked," he tells her. "We sent a crew."

PART II
Surge Season

8

ALTITUDES

THE FLYING pallets outside the garage are easily explained. Turns out the big warehouse that makes drone arms, just up the block: they left a stack of pallets outside their loading dock. They hadn't tied the pallets together, or discarded them, or done anything beyond leaving them dangerously alone. Like Revo, the drone-arm people weren't expecting the first surge to arrive a month early. The pallets were cheap. They were crafted perfectly for one-way flights. In the morning, the Strip District is littered with nail-filled hello's.

Leah and RedGill4 were not hit by pallets, though—or smashed by a falling delivery drone, or by some box that bounced off a flatbed, through a newly constructed bridge gutter, and then off the overpass.

It was a telepole. The RedGill had stopped at a swaying red light. Suddenly, the vehicle accelerated. The aerial detection system saw a threat, and the car opted to break a traffic law in the name of preservation. It saw the surge pushing the telepole. The car's calculation: *go*.

But RedGill4 chose the wrong direction. It would've been safer to jet backwards. The system couldn't predict the telepole would get tugged at an angle, toward the crosswalk. Various airborne electrical wiring had a say in things. The sidewalk was poured in a different century. The dented earth had cracked its knuckles a million times since the concrete was laid. Throw in a nervous delivery drone suctioned to the pole like a mechanical mosquito, and that two-story splintery bastard was more or less magnetized to the RedGill's trunk. It caught the prototype speeding through the intersection like a mouse in a trap.

Or at least that's how it all sounds the next morning coming from Dellinger, whose pointy ears jiggle as he talks. He fires off so many details that his ears become hexagonal kites bobbing in a surge. His ears really do seem to have points. Maybe it's how you become smart: your ears are wide enough to collect more info than the average engineer, and they're also sharp enough to pierce info as it floats by. Height helps, too. In the gray hallway to the garage, Dellinger's mop is higher than the blue Revo logo on the wall.

Yet despite his hyper intelligence and his 6'3", maybe 6'4" stature, Dellinger is such a sad-looking goober. It's the eyes. They frown. He talks so fast, and it's like he's constantly trying to give those brown eyes of his a little pep, a spark. He'd be handsome if he'd just pause. He *is* handsome—there's just too much chatter and gesture for anyone to really look at him. His big hands construct diagrams. He claps his fingers down onto his palm, explaining to Pegs that the pole crunched the trunk and the rear windshield. The clear helmet around the lidar kept the pole from doing pottery with Leah's brain.

"I was home," Dellinger tells her. "I freaked. I ran so fast to the elevator that this old rich couple thought I was a firefighter."

"Were you in a helmet or something?"

Dellinger paces in the long tunnel of a hallway. He explains how fast he was moving, rushing, sweating. So many freaking people kept getting on the elevator, the whole way down. Twice, he says "longest ride of my life." Pegs asks what happened to the RedGill.

"They saved the relevant tech."

"Define relevant." She can say this sort of stuff with Dellinger. With Yabner? No way. Yabner would say "What would you know about it?" Or: "What, are you creating an inventory of stuff you'd like to steal?" Dellyboy's big hands point at his own neck. He explains that the breakdown crew retrieved everything "from the neck up," meaning the car's lidar, the lidar helmet, basically all the non-car stuff.

"Did we retrieve anything I need to fix?"

Dellinger shrugs. "It's rip and wrap."

"Wrap?"

"We don't want pictures."

Pegs sidesteps two guys from Hardware. The metal sheet they're carrying is huge. It's like a bedspread for robots. Dellinger begins walking with them to the garage, and Pegs tells him to hang on. She asks again where the actual car wound up. The Dellinger Shrug: Coming To An AV Future Near You. She tells Dellinger she would have liked to try and save the vehicle, to rehab it, for the company, cost savings, a fun project. Dellinger explains that once the rear windshield shattered, rain filled the interior.

But: God bless Dellyboy. He cannot abide an unanswered question. If someone has a curiosity, he'll follow it, a lanky, hyper hound on a meaningless scent.

Delly stops the next person who passes. It's an electrical engineer, from Hardware. The guy sets down his crate of of wires, cables, and what Pegs can now recognize as an oscilloscope, a portable EKG-looking box that measures voltage and debugs circuitry. Who taught her about oscilloscopes? No one. It isn't a teaching type of industry. There's no point teaching someone to fish when you can financially leverage your abilities as a fisherman. The guy is in shorts, and you could shave every sleepless jaw in Revo with whatever tendon is bulging in his legs. It's like his calves have hard-ons. Dellinger is too tall to notice this sort of thing. Dell asks the guy if he was on the breakdown crew, where the prototype wound up.

"You don't have clearance," says Calves.

"I'm a Team Lead."

Boner Calf lifts his box. A cable tumbles overboard. He walks, dragging it. "Can Leads lift? There's more stuff."

"It's a simple question," Dellinger says.

"I don't talk with Leads without going through my own."

"I'd ask your Lead myself," Dellinger says, "but he's going to be hiding under his station all day."

Boner Calf hoists the black crate to his chest. "My sister's an executive psychiatrist," he says. "You want me to get you in? Is the crash getting to you?"

The two men continue like this, down the hall. Dellinger reiterates rank—he's a Lead, he has a right to know, the wreck wasn't his team's fault. The electrical guy with the calves keeps asking what it is exactly that Dellinger is even up to at the present moment, do you Systems people even work, what's your assign right now, loitering?

Pegs wishes she could freeze the pair. She wishes she could stick a needle in their skulls and extract the information she needs, namely: did the breakdown crew look in Leah's trunk? Were there random stolen parts laying around, randomly?

Pegs winds up following them to the garage. She doesn't acquire a single scrap of relevant gossip on the way. The remaining eleven prototypes are dozing in their three color-coded rows. The two hundred employees, meanwhile, are awake and then some. Everyone is in for the all-staff. What's more, seemingly half the sub-teams are moving semi-permanently from the computer part of the building into the garage now that surge season has apparently arrived. Surges do not wait for weekly updates and installs. Surges do not create the same predicable driving conditions in which the cars have been rehearsing for a decade-plus. The new aerial-perception product might very well require recalibrations after every single test drive in a surge, so there's a Vision sub-team from Software laying claim to every outlet at the rolly standing desk between BlueGill3 and 4. It's the same story with the Cybersecurity folks at the desk by the supply room. If everyone were to spread themselves out, there'd be ample room for each employee to have some personal space in the garage, and yet every single person attaches themselves to a cluster. The guys from Systems are ransacking a coffee cone by Pegs' work bench, and they all speak in perfect soundbites. Everything they say is sharp and seemingly unalterable, like diamonds. The current topic: should shelter alerts be triggered more easily year round. One guy says the standard needs to be kept high, otherwise society will shut down, constantly. By society it's pretty clear he means 'stuff I like to do.' Another guy says the formula they use for shelter alerts underrepresents change in wind velocity and overrepresents average wind speed. There's debate as to whether Revo should stream their drives now that the company will be sending drivers out into surges. Live ads could be sold.

"It's untapped revenue," says a bearded guy who hops to sit on Pegs' work bench. "Everyone's just at home watching stuff. Plus it would show the aerial perception upgrade is ready."

"Is it?" says Plasticky Glasses.

"It would differentiate us." Beard lifts a dead-blow mallet. He sets it down on the other side him, far from where he found it.

"One bad moment," says Glasses, "and we will get memed into the sun. Some kid on social comm will grab a flying dumpster or some driver sleeping and it will become the international symbol for tech failures."

"We should *want* to be an international symbol."

"Yeah, of *good* stuff."

No one asks Pegs whether her drives should be livestreamed. No one notices how nervous she is. She walks calmly to the supply room. No one is inside, performing inventory. She turns the light off, shuts the door, and locks it behind her back. She inhales sharply when she realizes that the Head of Content has been watching her. Thankfully, the woman decides that there's no video or podcast series to be culled from Pegs' fishiness. The Head of Content and her assistant make a similar assessment about the Hardware team congregating in front of the GreenGills: the pair of women record-then-delete a video of the men debating how best to re-fortify the exterior of the garage doors. The Hardware folks are arranging the huge metal sheets against the much larger metal exits, approximating how many sheets they'll need to cover it. Leaned upright against the garage door, the 6'x6' metal sheets look like projector screens. In Driver's Ed, cars crash on those sheets of metal. It reminds Pegs of her pre-teen summers.

Her mother would borrow a projector from the school she worked at. Pegs' cousin would rig a VHS to play *Star Wars* on the garage door at the bottom of the sloped driveway. That school has since flooded, and Pegs' cousin married a girl who once said, "The Force is anti-Christian."

A hand grabs Pegs' elbow. It's Smith. He's from Vision. Or Lidar. He's from something Software-based. Pegs holds her breath in her chest. She expects him to say: *So why exactly did they find a power inverter in the trunk of that Leah girl's RedGill? Plus side mirrors? Quite a haul.* But he just smiles. He lets go of her elbow. He says he's glad the wreck wasn't too hard. He's glad she didn't need a cast.

Pegs returns to the hallway as though there's some task waiting for her out there. There isn't. She creeps back to the doorway to check on GreenGill4. Boltz and Stomanovich from Software are leaning on the trunk. The flex pipes are still inside. So are the modular car batteries. Pegs can't remember every item she and Anna loaded in. She knows Anna never drove the parts to Lester's. Neither of them had a free moment to return everything to the supply room, what with the flying pallets, Leah crashing, the entire company turning the garage into a kind of vehicular military hospital as the cars prep for war. Some Revo employees really do seem to be treating the all-staff as a battle cry. They seem maniacally focused on how best to confront this huge looming human-historical climate problem that they and their technology have been presented with. Boner Calf has turned his crate upside down so his oscilloscope can sit on top. Dellinger is between two RedGills arguing about which routes should be tested first.

Yet other employees are less...active, less engaged. They're standing at the same literal sea-level as their peers, yet it's as though their brains are cruising at lower, safer altitudes. Boltz and Stomanovich are still leaning on GreenGill4, and Pegs swears the duo is projecting a shruggy indifference toward the whole circus unfolding around them. It's as though they'd like to convey to every clique in the garage that hey, um, if this whole aerially-reinforced lidar thing doesn't hit, we can work just as hard on the next pivot, the next company even, we're flexible. Yabner is touring the garage checking every coffee cone for creamer. He offers an enthusiastic fist bump here and there on the off chance that the CEO might walk down the hallway and witness Yabner in the act of team building. It's possible the CEO will enter from the exterior to give his speech. It's possible it's more of a check-in than a speech. Pegs doesn't really know the itinerary for the all-staff. She doesn't know much about the CEO, period. She knows that, according to a broad coalition of employees ranging from Leah to Yabner, the guy is too meek to lead his own piss to a toilet bowl. She knows he has the names of the AV Five tattooed on his scrawny shoulder blade, but this isn't some kind of special knowledge she gleaned from a seedy rendezvous. Everyone knows about the tattoos because every tech magazine and local newspaper profile snap a picture of him in an A-frame shirt. He yanks the strap aside to reveal the cursive names of people who died because of some rogue AV in 2023 or '26 or whenever, he's so motivated to change AV, to be safer in the third or fourth AV generation they're in, and now, with our new aerial approach…

The sound behind her in the hallway is not the CEO. It's not a pillaged coffee cone. It's Leah, flanked by Anna. Leah's sling is the only stationary thing about her. Her rain jacket: covering only one arm, the rest flapping behind her like the gray cape of some dolphin-themed heroine. Her red galoshes: marching toward the garage. Her chapped lips: forty paragraphs deep into a one-sided argument with Anna. Pegs jogs to her, interrupts: "Did they find the parts?"

"No, it's not broken," Leah says. "Yes, it was scary. I would love vodka, how kind."

"Did they look in the trunk?"

"They couldn't wrap it fast enough," Leah says. Pegs surveys her. She's in one piece. Leah's tracking dots have confirmed that Leah has been home and slept; Anna confirmed as much via phone calls; vibe-wise, it's as though Leah just stepped out of the totaled RedGill. It's like she's still waiting to give something a hard retributive kick. She seems coiled. The sling looks rigid, excessively so. It seems like it belongs on someone smaller. It's like they gave it to the wrong person.

"Do you want a glove or something?" Pegs asks. "For under the strap?"

"The whole car was just sitting there," Leah says. She does not stomp a red galosh. Her whole body is planted rigidly in front of Pegs, a human stomp. "Neither of you picked up."

Anna reiterates surge service, the booms. It's refreshing to see someone else take the lead re: being frustrated with Leah. It feels like Pegs is getting PTO right there in the hallway. Anna asks Leah: for the hundredth time, what would you have wanted us to do?

"Did they bring it here?" Leah heads for the garage.

"Dellinger said the inside was ruined," Pegs says.

Leah stops short of the doorway. She turns. "I'm aware."

Leah points at her sling, repeatedly. It's like she's jabbing a nickel-sized button that refuels her. "Water, through the back. Glass, through the back."

"You stayed inside?" Anna says.

"I couldn't see the pole!"

Pegs asks for the timeline—the crash, how long was Leah alone, when did the breakdown crew arrive, was there a tow, cops. Leah pauses. It's not a dramatic, fake, theatrical pause. It's a pause that suggests she is replaying the scene in real-time in her mind—the ambulance lights, EMTs talking to her, the breakdown crew disentangling computer from car, the sound and feel of rain. Leah inflates her chest. It's like she's trying to rise up larger and scarier-looking than the hard small rotten feeling in her stomach. She says she was getting in the ambulance when the crew started wrapping the prototype.

Tools rev. Guys from hardware are pre-drilling holes in the protective metal sheets. They're way up by the Green-Gills, but the noise is bouncing off the garage doors.

Pegs moves the drivers further away from the garage. Anna asks about the GreenGill, in the garage, from the night before, if Pegs had a chance to unpack it.

"It's safer getting that GreenGill to Lester's," Pegs says, "than those parts to the supply room."

"I'm done delivering," Anna says. She points. "It's packed in there."

"Which is why we can't unload here."

Anna zips her jacket. She lowers the zipper below her neck. "The parts are not a problem if we can get them back into the supply room."

"Half the sub-teams brought their laptops," Pegs says. "They might bring beds."

Anna peeks in the garage. She surveys the Hardware team drilling holes. "They realize the door might not open with those metal panels on it, right?"

"Tell them," Pegs says. "They love input."

Leah does not look to assess the door reinforcement process in the garage. She doesn't scan to see if Pegs' claim about beds is literal or another hyperbolic lie meant to put Anna on her heels. Leah stands so that both Anna and Pegs have to face her. Rain is still siphoning off her rain jacket. The concrete around her is constellated with surge water.

"We can get a car," Leah says. "I'm telling you." Leah shoos the coffee cone with her good hand. It drives a parallel line beside her trail of water while Leah drives arguments straight at Anna and Pegs. It's hard to keep up with her. In one sentence, she's talking about crashing at predetermined locations. The next, she's talking about staking out a dump. It's as though her mind is whirring into overdrive to compensate for her arm.

"A car is more complicated than parts," Pegs says.

"It's more parts," Leah replies.

Pegs lists all the *more* on her fingers: cars are tracked more militantly. They have more easily-traced parts. A car cannot fit in a trunk. Pegs would need a workspace, a big one. Whereas the parts have been new, the car would be used, likely damaged, perhaps severely.

"I'm aware," Leah says.

"Would we be trying to wreck?" Anna holds her high jacket zipper. It's like she's got a monocle or magnifying glass. "Or are we merely capitalizing on one?"

Leah asks why it matters. Anna says: because it does. She unzips her rain jacket. Her eyes scan several thousand bad occurrences. She looks as though she is skimming every report ever written in human history, be it automotive, medical, or tenth-graders summarizing *Huck Finn*. As quietly as she can while still being heard over tools, she outlines the many problems she sees when it comes to self-crashing a prototype. Anna says they would be endangering so many innocent people. If they're wrecking prototypes on purpose, and if people haven't safely sheltered yet, then they're endangering—

"How is that different than any other drive?" Leah says.

"Generally," Pegs replies, "I don't choose poles as destinations."

"Right, you choose apartments."

The weather in the garage changes. People stir. There's excitement. The drivers walk into the garage, and they discover that the CEO has appeared. He has done so in email form. The entire company bows their eyes and brains to read his "Our Moment" email in quiet unison. The CEO—who never does show—reminds the staff that this is the final push. It's now or never, although the never part is never said.

For however long this surge season lasts, the CEO writes, *Revo will prove, day in and day out, that our unparalleled aerial perception is more adept at recognizing weather-born dangers than the average driver, than our competitors, and than any mobility venture in human history. When society is ready for us, we'll be ready for them.*

9

DRONE ON DRONE

THERE ONCE was a man named Jason.
Or Jack.
Jon is possible, as is John.
This brown-haired J-man had handled Pegs' new employee onboarding. A year later, for her driver training, he and Pegs were the only two humans in the glass conference room. On both occasions, he had PowerPoints. He did not stress when a technical mishap caused a projection issue. Jay-John's entire vibe: technical problems are less important than our reaction to them. His vibe was also very food- and meeting-related. On "mental health" days that Pegs never received emails about, Jason-Jack could be found arranging lemon squares beside large artillery-esque coffee urns. His true calling seemed to be Social Gardener of the Glass Cube. Pegs often wondered if the guy ever left that impersonal space, though she did confirm he had personal items. In the most recent re-org, she'd seen Jon-John exit Revo with them.

All of this floods Pegs' memory when John-Jack pops onto the screen in the glass conference room. He is not live. He is pre-recorded. It seems possible that he's wearing the same shirt as the day he got canned from Revo. Across a two-hour retrain, Johnny-Jason tours Pegs through information she already knows.

Stay within the geofence, keep the cars below sixty-two degrees.

Phone usage lasting longer than 2.5 seconds will result in a disengagement. Here's how it works.

Passengers are prohibited unless they have completed training.

Yes, we know it's a bit odd to have a driver monitoring system surveil you when the goal is to have no one in the front seat at all, but we're merely complying with legislation made by people who do not understand us. Plus the cars are rather pricey, so.

Jimmy-Jack informs Pegs that the final part of her retrain is a driving test. The screen goes blank. No one enters the glass conference cube. No one is waiting for her in the hall. None of the employees in the busy garage volunteer to assess Pegs' retrain test. None seem to even know about it. They're all preoccupied. Even if someone did know about the retrain ride, it seems doubtful any brave soul would accompany her. Everyone in Revo is keen to obey the Shelter Alerts, which would be hard for even the most disruptive of five-year-olds to misinterpret. The gist of the text messages: Go inside. If you're inside, stay there.

Pegs' job, as a test driver during surge season, is simple: disobey these sheltering requests. She's incentivized to do so. Ten of her twenty test-driving hours must occur during surges. She receives a tidy $100 bonus for every full surge hour she completes beyond the mandatory ten. So: if she's home and it starts surging? She starts test driving. If she's rotating the tires on a RedGill? She zips her spandexy

Revo rain jacket and hits the road. The Shelter Alerts are like a starter's pistol. Everyone else leaves the track, she jumps on. Once she's out in the rainy world, she waits.

She waits for a drone to crash onto her rain-pounded windshield.

She waits for her inflatable seat belt to explode.

She waits for Leah's telepole to sprout legs and hunt her down.

She waits to see any other human driver out on the roads. She rarely does. The cars brake at stop signs for no real reason. It's not like anyone ever crosses. The traffic lights are more decorative than necessary, as though the city decided to decorate for Christmas in late October.

The only vehicles she meets at red lights are driverless prototypes from Norroyo and Ryde. The test drivers are all grim-faced in the day-round windy darkness. The Norroyo vehicles seem small. The Ryde seats are very...forward. The woman test driving the six-wheel Ryde looks like she's sitting in a cupboard. Pegs wonders what her surge bonus is like, how many hours it takes. She wonders where the girl lives, is it close, affordable, high, worse than Pegs' spot or better. She doubts any of them have a Lester.

Although at this point, Pegs barely has a Lester.

She pulls into an empty parking garage, midday. She disables the system and drives herself up into the concrete belly. The rain is blown all the way to where she parks. She checks the LedgerCoin account. The last payment Lester uploaded was for wheels. She still hasn't divvied it. She hasn't dropped off a single new item since surges started, nor have Leah and Anna. She looks at the payment. It'll be a fight—$22.75, are you serious, it's so little, we need more, why haven't you figured out a way to get us a car, you're the car person, don't you know that Anna has loans, and that your apartment is going to flood, and that Leah wants a new civilization?

Pegs opens Dots, the private location tracking app the three drivers use. Anna blinks her way through Sheraden. Leah, after only five days of comp time, is back out on a route. It's possible she's busing to work. Or: she's out protesting, waving her sling on an empty surge-walloped boulevard.

Pegs initiates a new route. She exits the parking structure into guess what: rain. The side windows get hit just as bad as the windshield. It feels as though she's the last person alive in the city, winding through the wind- and rain-hammered roads. If regular traffic is a kind of snake, she's a brand new baby snake, unable to grow beyond a single unit.

Or: she is a mouse, free to roam amid the snakeless chaos of the surge, which is all-encompassing, immersive, engulfing. It's like she's being driven inside an upset stomach. The stomach is digesting wind. The first week, the surges come without warning—gray sky, blue sky, black, doesn't matter. It's the fourth year in a row. It might be the fifth. No one wants to use the word hurricane. The city doesn't get hurricanes. It and several other Appalachian areas are experiencing surges. Temporarily. For four straight years, maybe five, a condition in which it seems to pour every hour. By her fourth shift, she swears every gutter is clogged. Rain spills down from two and three stories in loud unfiltered streams. On every block, it's as though there are multiple mini-skies dumping their own mini-surges. The city's 446 bridges are the world's most rundown, yellow-painted irrigation system. Some of their gutters pour into one of the three rivers. Other fabricated channels guide the overflow away from underpasses and houses, toward unbuilt areas that become slop.

The wind is the real problem, though. Anything without a foundation winds up in the street. Traffic cones topple about as though kicked. Street signs lay in crosswalks. Any standalone object gets shoved about by fifty invisible hands. Doesn't matter how durable it is. On a wet day run, Pegs and BlueGill2 get walloped by an empty trash barrel. On a clear dusk drive, she comes across a porch awning in the street, aluminum. The BlueGill traces a path around the broken beak-like thing with ease. The car is more cautious with the metal For Sale sign in Swisshelm Park. The signage part crawls across Whipple Street in the wind. It drags the wooden post behind it. There's no point calling the number—it's a house, not an apartment. Plus the commute from Swisshelm would be brutal. It actually might not be bad what with shelter alerts, less traffic. Once the sign drags itself halfway across, the BlueGill scoots past.

Trees are harder to avoid. The wind bends their bare limbs toward her, all day, and every time, Pegs so badly wants to seize the wheel and steer the prototype onto a safer, emptier street. The solo dogwoods don't stand a chance. They get uprooted with ease. The endless groves in Schenley Park can distribute the wind more evenly; they tend to lose only branches, until suddenly, out of nowhere, clouds surround the car, blinding it. They seep inside the interior. Oxygen disappears. Her seatbelt has no button. It binds her to the seat. The clouds have transfigured the air conditioning into a kind of wet-cement slop. Her nose, lips, and chin push and prod at the weather. She swallows lightning. She throws her chest against the seat belt. It inflates like thunder. The software won't trigger an alert, won't help, won't save her. She keeps waiting for an Inattentive, a Disengagement. The car won't respond. Someone is in the backseat. They speak. Hands shake her.

It's her sister. Avery is standing above the bed, dripping onto the mattress. "The window's leaking."

The kitchen lights are blinding. Pegs can hear the water before her eyes adjust. It's like the glass block is a wooden keg; someone has stuck a knife where it meets the wall. The leak isn't pouring, but it's steady, a good trickle. Avery has stationed a long rectangular Tupperware on the ground. A black cutting board is angled in an attempt to direct water from the wall to the basin. It isn't working. The wall is soaked. Thin rivers explore the tile.

"I couldn't find the caulk gun," Avery says.

"It's got to be dry."

"Better than nothing."

Pegs brings towels from the bathroom. Avery says they're clean. Pegs dumps them on the floor. Avery says she left a message with the super.

Pegs zips her Revo coat. She stomps into rain boots. "He's not driving in a surge."

She opens the pantry and kicks aside wiper fluid and dust pans. She wraps the work belt around her waist, latches two hammer drills onto the strap, and tests the flashlight on the carpeted stairs. When she opens the front door, rain blankets half the lobby.

She hangs a right outside the brick building and heads downhill. Water rushes down the tilted street. There's a hearty creek flowing along the sidewalk, an inch deep, maybe more. A full quarter mile of sloped Edmond Street is funneling down onto her building. She swears the water is scooting innocently past the fifty row houses on either side, then blasting the fortress she built around her low glass-block window. Water splashes off the massive truck tires she sawed in half and drilled together in a stack. They're drilled into the sidewalk and both sides of the window. Plywood seals the top.

But the bottom is no longer sealed. The protective stack she made has been uprooted. She shines her light on the sidewalk. Water is coursing underneath the bottom tire. Her light catches on the blue head of a Tapcon screw beneath the rainwater. The screw is drilled into the sidewalk and nothing else. There's been a tear, or a slip job.

She feels along the bottom loose tire and her fingers find a squishy stick of some kind glued to the bottom tire. It feels like a lightly insulated spinal cord belonging to some hand-sized animal. She tears it free, curses—it's a line of hardened caulk. She should've let the caulk dry an extra day in the crack before drilling the tires to the sidewalk. The tire has ripped it out. Some force has ripped it out, at any rate. She lowers her chin to the rush of water and shines her light beneath the tires. Her sweatpants sponge up every water molecule on long downhill Edmond Street. Neither the rubber nor caulk are protecting the crack below the window. The plywood doesn't reach all the way down. Water rushes in, unabated.

A squeak echoes inside the tires. She flinches, recoils. She swears she can see some sort of shadow inside. A creature is living in her creation. It could be multiple. She should've built a second layer of half-tires around the initial three. She envisions rat piss and squirrel feces leaking down the cutting board.

She stands and kicks the stack of rubber. The fort bounces

in the water where it's off the screw. No animal scurries out. She fires one of the hammer drills blindly down into it and swears she hears a howl, a yelp. She triggers again, but nothing tries to bite the whirling carbide bit. She hears another yell, and it is not from inside the tires. It's from higher on Edmond Street. Through the rain, she can see kids wakeboarding. They have started up on Liberty Avenue and are enjoying one long, uninterrupted ride down Edmond Street. Each board has a small brushless motor on the back, helping the boys glide with force right toward her apartment.

She waves her light, airing it out like a huge white sheet in the rain. The boys don't obey the signal. They don't change course to the street. They choke up on their wrist reins and gain speed. One crouches into himself. He hops airborne off a rise in the asphalt, splashes to earth, and rushes past her. A second full-body red rain suit follows him.

Pegs leaps from the water to the building's stoop. The three remaining boarders take aim at her. They crouch. They trace along the stoop's edge and veer toward the apartment building. The first rider uses the tire fortress as a kind of side bumper. He flashes his board against the rubber and springs off, the tires fluttering winglike in his wake. The second rider yanks on his rein and leaps. He doesn't quite clear the top, but he lands fast and straight on the other side.

The smallest boy, in goggles: he catches the stack all wrong. His board wedges somewhere low in the three tires and his body soars downhill with such speed that his wrist strap pulls the wakeboard from the tires. Perhaps the small river of water provides him some cushion against the concrete. Keyword: some. The kid moans vowels on the walk, alone.

Pegs jumps from the stoop, picks up the board, tosses it uphill behind herself, and kneels. She flattens the thick wrist strap against the sidewalk and holds it in place with her rain boot. She tests the drill, then fires the long carbide bit through the water, strap, and concrete.

The drilling is loud and then some, a high-pitched witch biting the big one in a power blender. The boy sits up and recoils. His arm writhes, a dog at the end of its chain. Pegs is the stake. She sits on the strap. She bows her legs to divert water, to keep her work area dry. The bigger problem is the board, which keeps motoring into her back. The rain keeps coming, too. Her sweat pants are more water than fabric. There's also the issue of the boy not really wanting to be fastened to the sidewalk. He yanks the strap. Pegs kicks his hand. She grabs a Tapcon screw from her pocket, the second drill from her belt, and fires the screw sloppily into the walk.

The boy jerks against the screw. He's got about two feet of slack. She shines the light in his eyes. His face is so white he's glowing. "Leave the board," Pegs tells him.

"This is two hundred bucks."

"You've been tearing my shell."

"It wasn't us."

"It just literally was."

The boy yanks the strap, but it stays drilled in the walk. He pulls himself up the street as though he's dangling from a cliff and climbing to safety. Pegs debates drilling a second screw but doesn't want to ruin the strap anymore than she has. What she wants is for the kid to unlatch and let go of the damn wrist thing. There's a hefty worm on the

kid's neck. He's being parasited. It's a tattoo. The stenciled
words are too cursive to be read. "My arm is broken," he
says.
"You yanked the strap," Pegs says. "Go shelter."
"How am I supposed to get home?"
It's a good question, one Pegs thinks about as she drags
the wakeboard up Edmond Street the next surge-less
morning. She doesn't find the kid sleeping on some aw-
ning-protected stoop in Yew Street or Lima Way. He's not
nursing a broken hand outside the bookstore or anywhere
else on flat busy Liberty Avenue. There's no comfortable,
un-itchy way to Velcro the wakeboard's strap around her
wrist. She ends up pulling it like a sled. The scraping isn't
quite nails on a chalkboard. It's more like chalk on chalkboard, one endless straight line drawn across a chalkboard
the size of Bloomfield. For a cold November day, the ac-
tivity is wild. Every dog on the planet is out and active.
They're like arrowheads on the end of their leashes. Two
mail carriers work the block. She searches Rūm for the
apartment being advertised above the thrift store. A single
room is going for $1,900, starting November fifteenth.
There's odd language about when it's permissible to use
the kitchen and bathrooms.
The wakeboard knocks the telepole. She's surprised it
doesn't fall on her. Things are not working. She almost says
it aloud. Two women are power walking toward her, re-
leasing god knows how many straight days of energy, and
she feels the urge to share every stressor with them. The
women seem to notice her. They sense her despondency.
They're looking right at her. Their conversation stalls.
The women have kind eyes. Pegs would start by explaining the wakeboard, the tire fort. She would say how she'd

love to live higher, but it's too expensive. It's been hard to hit surge bonuses what with the cars requiring more maintenance. It's been difficult to move parts. The garage is packed. Lester's business is slow now that fewer people are driving. Her sister's coffee shop is closed four, sometimes six days a week now. Her surge pay ain't cutting it. Nothing is. Leah wants a full car, but it's a fantasy, she'd tell the women, then she'd ask about theirs. Maybe the two normal-seeming women are currently experiencing their fantasy—a walk with company.

The only company Pegs receives arrives via her phone. She checks it once the women pass.

Leah has complaints about the tire payment.

Anna responds.

Revo wants her to come in.

The texts sit on her head the rest of her walk down Liberty Ave. She feels like the prototypes she rides around in: navigating the city while carrying a heavy technological weight. She passes a billboard—a five-o-clock shadow in a hardhat. He's got an open beer raised at an angle, about to drink. Delivery drones pass across the can like a saw in a magician's act, and for reasons she can't explain, she has the sense that everything is just so…high now. Telepoles, apartments, roof-riding aerial lidar helmets, aluminum cans on billboards—everything is above her. She breathes. She tries to picture everything as existing below her, lower than even the wakeboard. That's how the world once was. That's how the city was, at any rate. Steel used to reside in the earth. It used to burble below, then Pittsburghers raised it to the living world. Now, steel robot eyes got welded to your car roof. The steel robot eyes were needed to protect against all the steel flying through the sky. This roofy steel also communicated with steel satellites that spent their days orbiting the once steel-filled planet.

It occurs to her that satellites probably aren't steel. Nor are the lidar helmets. Steel wasn't really ever in the earth. The whole process has to do with iron or ore, coke, stuff her grandparents knew about and did. The point is that things used to be underfoot, and now, they're overhead. So many airborne items feel like they could crash on her, at any moment. The worst part is that the crash never comes. She lives beneath a steel wave. She's forever encysted in this pre-drown panic.

The high bells ring when she enters. They ring again when she yanks the wakeboard into the pawn shop. She drags the board through the tables and displays of junk. Three items are highlighted above the workbench behind the glass barrier:

1) an auto-painter, hung on the wall like some kind of droopy mechanical spider.

2) some blue guitar that is evidently quite a catch.

3) the coffee cone from Pegs' pantry.

"Two grand?" Pegs says. "You gave me twenty bucks."

The redhead turns his head but not his back. His hands continue tinkering. Every tool from his bag is littered across his workbench. "I gave you five-hundred and forty dollars. Exactly."

"I want another hundred if it sells for two."

"Is that board a Konda?"

It's not. She removes the wrist bracelet. "It's in good shape."

"Looks beat."

"It's durable."

"There's a gun shot. In the strap."

"It's for your thumb." She sticks hers in. Her knuckle won't pass the hole. The guy tells her he needs a minute. He says he's close. There's a snap of some kind. It sounds partway between plastic and metal. He curses.

Pegs stands the board against the plexiglass. The better value is store credit, not cash, but nothing leaps out. She palms the dome of a parking meter. It wouldn't be worth cracking open to see what's left. Lamps are lamps. Black Steelers jerseys hang like animal skins, the numbers bone white. She lifts a metal T. It's a boating tie-off. She feels like she's heard the word *cleat* before. Boats dock on them in seasons that don't require rain jackets as thick as space suits.

Pegs lifts two T's. She could drill four into her building, one on each corner of the low glass block window. She doesn't know what she'd drape across them or fix to them. She doesn't see anything else of use. The refrigerator door is too big. The historic plaques in a box are too small. One is from some bank. Another is from Point State Park, where the three rivers meet. The write-up outlines the land's lineage. Indians, Brits, the French. Virginians, Pennsylvanians. There's no mention of the water that now climbs the steps. The computer section is a waste.

"How about window shields?" she asks.

The redhead says "Ow." He's talking to whatever object is hurting him. He's cooing, tsking. "The shields really go."

"I'd like to spend my one clear day outside."

The redhead consents. He drops a tool on the bench and exits his plexiglass prison to investigate the board. His workbench looks like a battlefield. The war was between two mechanical nations. Two soldiers are locked in battle, dead.

It's drones. It's the closest she's ever been to them. They're usually on a console screen, up high. The arms look strong enough to squeeze the organs out of her. The grayer one has pierced the darker one. It has hunted it down. It's as though the gray one is patiently waiting for evolution to grant it a mouth so it can swallow what it caught.

"This isn't a Konda," says the redhead.

Pegs knocks the plexiglass. "Drones fight?"

"Came in yesterday." The red head continues his assessment of the board. Pegs lowers her face to the square hole in the plexiglass. An arm from the gray drone is all the way through the brainy body of the dark one. An arm from each is braided together.

"Are there fighting leagues or something?"

"In a surge," says the redhead, "they cling to whatever's closest."

10

WOMAN, ASTRIDE SANDBAGS

PEGS ACQUIRES three things at the pawn shop:
1) A bundle of fives in exchange for the wakeboard;
2) The aching sense that she and her sister won't be able to afford any move, anywhere, ever;
3) Worse nerves about the delivery drones.

For a week afterward, her foot never strays too far from the brake. She quickly learns that it's not natural to drive with one's sneaker tensely shadowing the brake. God, does her ankle get sore. It's like playing the old Operation game from her parents' basement, except she's playing it for five hours and doing so with her toes. Her black rain-boot doesn't hover for all five hours, but it does any time she spots a delivery drone out in the windy weather. She wishes she'd never seen the arms up close. Their size is unsettling. Whenever she spots a mess of them in the air, it's hard to look elsewhere. She finds herself waiting for the drones to swerve or dive. She waits for the screen to bleat redly, to say: DISENGAGED, *you're on your own, we can't see what's falling, actually scratch that, three drones are arm wrestling on the roof to see who gets to squeeze your skull.*

These alerts never come. No drones fall. Every auto-mated item performs shockingly well in the surges, the

Revo prototypes included. Her RedGill stops cold right as
a mailbox springs off a row house as though drawn across
Sarah Street on a cheap wobbly string in some high school
play. When BG4 hydroplanes on a curvy part of Beech-
wood Boulevard, the system doesn't panic; the helmeted
lidar keeps the car driving the perfect angle, as though it
were a toy being guided through the water by an unusually
responsible toddler. The emails she receives are so...posi-
tive. None mention Leah's wreck. They do mention how a
test driver has been able to operate a vehicle one-handed,
which is yet another great sign for the disability commu-
nity. The emails make it seem as though licensing is right
around every wet corner. Every day, the whole company
gets to hear about some new milestone they've collectively
achieved. The company sets internal records for most miles
driven while in "Near Gale" and "Strong Gale" conditions.
The company celebrates an alert-free twenty-four hours
while the skies set a state record—fourteen inches of rain.

The text messages are less enthusiastic. They fit two cat-
egories:

1) Lester paying her a pittance for parts he recently
moved;

2) Leah and Anna complaining about the even smaller
pittance Pegs has sent them.

The worst of it is that neither kind of text is all that fre-
quent. Loading parts into the trunks is impossible. Every
single Revo sub-team works nonstop. The surges have sent
them into Garage Mode, Quadruple Overdrive. Pegs can
never find a private moment. She certainly can't stash any
sellable objects in a trunk. She can never strategize with
Leah or Anna whenever they pull in from a drive. There's
been little conversation re: how to advance, up their take,

get a full car, a full set of tires even, anything. There's been little time or space to even think. The folding chair Pegs would love to collapse in is always occupied by some co-worker whose laptop is plugged into a prototype. When it's Stomanovich in the chair, he talks about movies. He's never concerned with acting or story, jokes or tears—none of that. He only cares about how right they got the technology.

Boltz only ever talks about the new gelato place on the first floor of his tall apartment building. The stuff is upsettingly bad, an insult to Italy, where he's been, multiple times. There are certain shifts where Pegs swears Boltz says *stracciatella* seven times per minute. Somewhere— freaking Italy, presumably—the guy got it in his head that culture or cachet or whatever was merely a matter of where your feet have been.

Content Kel, the marketing lead, takes photos of the cars when they come in from test drives. She sits in the chair fussing over the pictures like the images are show dogs, all while dressed in a kind of Utility Chic that suggests she's hosting a pricey webinar for aspiring mariners.

Yabner sits with his laptop and his brown-green smoothies from the caf. She swears they're his only calories these days. He's rather obviously obsessed with remaining as thin and young-seeming as his co-workers. The dude is sensitive about his age. Pegs doesn't help his sense of his self-worth. The mere presence of test drivers seems to symbolize to Yabner that he has failed. He hasn't been able to eradicate humans from driving. It's actually more like the world has failed to recognize and adopt Yabner's super amazing life efforts at various companies that have either been bought, merged, or evaporated. The result is

that Yabner is perpetually irked by Pegs. He's always nee-
dling her. Sometimes it's about the noisiness of a particular task she's doing. Other times, like when he approaches
her on Saturday evening, it's a more direct inquiry about
her very existence at the company: "What's your goal
here? You trying to get kept on at a service center?"

Pegs flips the switch on the hydraulic lift. The Green-
Gill's tires rise off the floor. "I was hoping to get out of my
basement before surge season."

"When they license these, you'll get a stock bump."

"I'm contract."

Yabner sips his smoothie. "You didn't negotiate stock?"

Pegs stops the lift when the GreenGill's tires reach her
shoulders. She tells Yabner that the tone in her brief inter-
view had been very team-oriented.

"They were desperate," Yabner says.

"That became apparent."

"Teams are bullshit." Yabner sips. "Every roboticist
knows it."

Pegs sits in the office chair. She rolls under the Green-
Gill. Add to the list of Revo-related grievances: there's
no mechanic's underworld. Even the country's most rat-
infested Jiffy Lube has an underground walkway. "Do you
honestly think they'll license these?" she says.

"Not if I spend half my day walking from my desk to
the garage." Yabner launches into his standard critique of
the CEO. Yabner says it's so unbelievably ridiculous for
the guy to force everyone to work in the garage, alongside the cars. The CEO's stupid theory is that working in
closer proximity to the cars will actually improve everyone's work, their sense of the stakes, their company-wide
bond. "Every middle-school science-club advisor tries to
get smart kids to work together," Yabs tells Pegs, "but it's

against the fundamental nature of what roboticists do. Roboticists aren't meant for teams, or unions, or any of this bunk-bed crap." Yabner tosses the smoothie cup at the trash. It's surprising how close he comes to actually making it in. Like most guys at Revo, he's the kind of person who doesn't think to wash the cup, take it to the cafe where Avery works, and, because it looks approximately like the cafe's cups, use it for a two dollar refill instead of a six dollar coffee.

It's a relief when Yabner's seat is filled by Raj. The relief evaporates when Raj sets an ashtray on the empty seat next to his. For the longest time, Raj had used the Revo-branded vape pens given out in the goodie bags at last summer's Software retreat. But the gossip is that Raj has been dumped. From the sounds of it, it's classic Revo stuff—she hated his long hours at work, his unwillingness to see boundaries there, the way in which his interest in work dwarfed his interest in her. Raj had vaped for his girlfriend, who hated the smell of cigarettes, and now that his girlfriend has left the picture, so too have the Revo-branded vape pens. Cigarettes are barred from the garage, yet Raj's superiors and peers seem unwilling to chastise him during this rough patch. Cigarette stubs poke up from his ashtray like some kind of albino octopus being suffocated in a bad beach. The smell makes it difficult for Pegs to get excited about the new apartment listing, available December 1st. It's in a smoking building.

"The hell is a 'raised first floor?'" Leah asks. It's hard to tell which aspect of the listing is most bewildering for her—the "raised" part, the app's interface, or her attempts to navigate Rūm with one arm in a sling. She hands the phone back to Pegs.

"They probably laid tile on tile," Pegs says.

"Two grand isn't awful."

Pegs turns the key, throws the hydraulic switch. The lift lowers BlueGill1 toward the concrete. "A first floor is a first floor."

"A raised floor, Peggles." Leah sweeps her sneaker beneath the tire. She sweeps it back through before the tire lands. "Maybe it's an apartment on a hovercraft."

Pegs can barely hear her over all the powertooling. Someone from Hardware is in a welder's mask. He's triggering a tool. It sounds like an ambulance being eaten by a garbage disposal. Finding flexible protection for the garage doors is apparently still proving to be difficult. It's the kind of nagging problem that can no longer be fit into anyone's regular schedule, hence the Saturday evening work. Huge Flexi-metal sheets are the current approach. They've been affixed to the outside of the doors. But when Door Four is raised, as a test, some metal corner snags. The door can't fully open. Some stray bit of the new shield is catching in the track.

The guys curse. They fire air and also fire out of their tools as old rain drips from the door. They try to lower it. The door won't drop. It sticks. There's an endless metallic hum.

"You can probably still get under that," Pegs says.

"I've met quota for regular hours," Leah says. "I need a surge." Leah points at the open door. It's wet and dark out, but it's not raining. "Listen," she says, "we need to talk."

Pegs declines, says she's behind. She's got to rotate the tires on every RedGill. A GreenGill has a cough. When it surges, she wants to drive. She needs this week's bonus. Her sister has been hit with Shelter Alerts on her last three shifts.

Leah walks under Door 4, out into the cloudy Saturday

evening. The girl is so incredibly frustrating. She doesn't debate. She just…does. By the time Pegs jogs out beneath the stalled grinding door and past the Hardware team cursing into their tools, Leah is slipping through the crash poles. She scuffs her way toward the cold river.

Pegs removes her safety glasses and pins them on her shirt. She spends so little time outside. The wet night air draws a brand new face on her. The sandbags are stacked five-high. It looks like it's only three-high in some spots, six in others. The line doesn't look wide enough to cover Revo's property.

Leah jumps up onto the barrier. Even in a sling, you can tell she's an athlete. She's not clumsy, at any rate. She looks to her right. The 31st Street bridge is small, way down the Allegheny. She points. "I've only seen this from the cars."

At first, Pegs sees only the bridge. Whereas other bridges have gutters that direct water off onto short wings, the 31st street Bridge has the kind with simple holes drilled in the side. There's no traffic or highway beneath it. It dumps water onto water. Right now, nothing falls from the drains. No boats draw on the river.

Then, from the other shore, bright red dots travel airborne across the Allegheny. They're single-file. The string of dots is maybe halfway between the bridge and where Leah stands. It's hard to tell. They're safe and high above the river. The line of red dots keeps growing.

The dots are delivery drones. They hew to the coordinates of their private invisible bridge, and when they reach the middle, they meet and pass another lane of themselves. Soon the dots blur and collide and become indistinguishable. For a while, it looks like the red lights are uniting then separating. Then, it looks like high collisions.

"Older models." Leah walks along the line of bags.

"They only cross when they're positive they don't need to suction."

Pegs listens for their droney hiss. The river eats the shore. "They spook me."

"It's all just flying toilet paper," Leah says.

"They're bigger than you'd think."

Pegs steps up onto the barrier. The sandbags are logoless. It's rare to see a surface without Revo's slashy font. She had heard the bags were branded, but that must have been a joke. She never thought to actually check. She's never looked beyond the barrier. There isn't much. The tiny shore is trashy. There are webs of ancient fishing line and rods broken into V's. In the flat spots, there are loose puddles and tight ones.

Leah bends. She checks a sandbag for a tag, a leak, who knows. It's like she's looking for a collar. "So, two things."

"Just two?" Here's how much Pegs appreciates the fresh air: it has taken her this long to realize how fishy the shore smells. It smells like mud-filled dead fish buried inside a tire. A big tire, 94R. She doesn't know what kind of fish. Fish fish.

Leah skips a rock. It sinks instantly. "The first is: we need help."

Pegs digs her heels into the sandbag. She digs her toes in, an eighth of an inch, maybe. It's a little concerning how easy it is to dent the bags. "You're in a sling, I'm selling wakeboards—I'd say we're doing just great on our own."

"There's wakeboards in there?"

Pegs shoos the bugs nesting between her glasses and shirt. She tells Leah it's a long story. Leah says hers is shorter: she wants to talk with drivers from Ryde. Talk as in: talk seriously. About collaboration. A second parts pipeline. So on. She wants Pegs to come with her. Leah knows two Ryde drivers, from protesting. She has gotten the sense that they aren't the only ones at Ryde who are losing faith. There's a software liason, a comms person. Half of Ryde is worried about getting canned. The whole six-wheel approach isn't going well.

"We can barely run our own thing," Pegs says.

"We need more heads on this," Leah says.

"More heads is less money." Pegs locates the rot that she's smelling. It's maggots in a bag of white bread. It was bread, at least. They look like hundreds of wiggling wire connectors. Pegs hits them with a rock, and suddenly river insects fly between she and Leah. The insects have likely been stampeding through the whole time. The bugs are surely racing under the half-open garage door to the unprotected prototypes. They're coating the cars, infesting them, licking the garage's high fluorescents, maybe forming into a long sentence for everyone to read: *The Drivers Are Strategizing Again, Beware.*

Leah brings her knees together. She crouches on a single bag. It seems unsafe to balance like that, what with the sling, the river. "I didn't talk to them yet because I knew you'd freak."

"I don't freak." Pegs refuses to breathe. She decides to prove that she doesn't overreact. It strikes her that suffocating oneself is an act of freaking.

"I completely get and respect that you've accomplished a lot on your own."

"Two more hours and I get a surge bonus." Pegs inhales as quietly as she can. "My first."

"Then what?"

"Then I'll try to get another." She tries to calculate how

many surge bonuses she would need to pay first and last at the smoking apartment with the "raised" floor. She'd have to pay out November at their current spot. There's likely a fee for breaking the lease. The thought makes her sit on a sandbag. She plugs her fingers beneath her thighs. "We'll get a steadier cash flow soon," she says. "Business for Lester will pick up."

"About that." Leah straightens, plants her sneakers on separate sandbags. She turns toward Revo, and the distant fluorescents bring out the white logo on her Revo rain jacket. A person with even a speck of artistic know-how would gather oils and pens and whatever arty crap was necessary to sketch a picture.

Woman in A Sling, Astride Sandbags, Pre-Storm.

Woman, Facing Employer, who says: "I switched the tow to Lester. He's getting the call for the next wreck."

The Allegheny slides off the shore. When it oozes back, it feels as though the water rises up Pegs' shins and thighs. The sandbag has fully soaked her butt. She accepts that her underwear is going to be soaked, all night. She accepts that when Lester sees her, he will chase her through Bloomfield, then Oakland, then maybe all the way down the Ohio River and Mississippi and into the Gulf. He'll be irate. He will attempt to secure her head in a filter wrench. Lester will be beyond furious to find himself in a formal business agreement with the company from which he is also selling hot parts.

Pegs starts a statement. She can't bend it into a question. "They would never choose Lester."

"Chose you out of Lester's," Leah says. "I told the marketing lady we need to increase local partnerships."

Pegs wishes there was a second line of sandbags behind

her. She wants to lean back, support herself, stare at nonexistent stars. Water spreads down her jeans. She tries to ignore it. "A car is very different than parts. Like, extremely."

"We talk ourselves sick," Leah says.

The drone highway is gone. Above the water, it's just a dark bridge, oily clouds. A surge seems unlikely. "What did Les say?"

Leah steps off the sandbags. "See, that's a *you* thing."

11

THE BEACON OF SOFT DRINK LANE

THE BOWLING alley is crowded, even for a Saturday without a shelter alert. The consistency of screaming and yelling is akin to indoor rain. The DJ cuts through the yelling, pins, and gutters to say the next three songs are for Connor. The DJ is not a visible person on a visible mic. It's a robotized program of some kind. It's unclear if Connor is real.

Pegs and Leah scan for Lester. Pegs doesn't scan all that hard. It's a nice change of pace—to wander, explore, be around non-Revo people. Her last social outing was... well, she wasn't technically "working" during the all-staff. She doesn't mind that the place smells like a casket lined with soggy popcorn, popcorn that's been dipped in polyurethane, though when she steps on a sticky spot, it is not the last one. There are multiple birthdays going on. Lester's adult daughter and her carcinogenic smile are in charge of the birthday gathering in Lane 11. Presents are open. The clear winner: the AI soldier equipped with a supersoaker. The soldier, two feet tall, is all rods and levers. It's got big, gasket-looking eyes. The birthday boy pours his soft drink into the weapon, then the contraption walks timidly at a small bowler debating balls. There's nothing timid about the way the contraption hoses the kid down with pop. It's a solid stream. The soldier staggers up toward the hardwood lane, which it sprays gratuitously.

Pegs scans to see if some responsible parent is readying a towel. Lester's daughter is out to lunch on her phone. An attending mom grabs a girl who's either a waitress or a janitor. The mom points at the soft drink pooling in the lane: *It's our fault, we'll regulate it better moving forward, but could you maybe.*

The waitress' smart watch blinks throughout the whole discussion. The alerts are from the CounterCash. It's sending orders to the girl's wrist. Pegs has heard her sister refer to "wearing a leash" at the cafe, and it really does seem as though the bowling-alley employee is being yanked toward the main counter, where a line has formed in front of a white CounterCash. The cylindrical things give Pegs the chilly willikens. They look like a sheet thrown over a small kid for Halloween. Their five red eyes form a circle, and as the girl darts in front of it on her quest to get a rag, she passes Lester, alone at a table. He's slurping pink lemonade through a straw. The plate of cookies looks untouched, as does the box of Legos. He touches his phone, constantly.

It takes a while for Lester to spot them. The look he gives says:

1) Jesus, you're robbing me, aren't you;

2) So long as you're quick, I don't care.

Pegs sits across from him. The rack of bowling balls is taller than her shoulder. She lifts the Lego box, an orange underwater explorer. "Nice wrap job."

Lester doesn't answer. He doesn't move. He looks at

Leah's sling but does not ask about it. Fear looks odd on him. He's usually so doglike. He's still as a cat.

"Christ on a cross," he says, "are you tracking my truck?"

"Your daughter posts a lot," Leah says. She lifts the plate of cookies. She transfers it from Lester's side to theirs. The cookies are pilgrims, turkeys. Leah bites tail feathers.

Lester holds his lemonade. He's getting his paws back, slowly. He points the empty straw at Leah, looks at Pegs. "I said no more busy Lizzie."

Pegs scrunches her legs underneath the teeny table. Bowling pins cluck and squawk. The machines that clean them are so quiet. You can barely hear them. It's possible that the DJ is just really, really loud. Pegs selects a cookie, bites a Pilgrim. "Which grandkid?"

"Anthony." Lester flinches at the volume of the new song. "Eight."

"Fun," Leah says.

"Entitled." Lester prods the deep-sea Lego with his fountain drink. "I'm supposed to manifest a scuba so they can blast it with that pisser."

Say this for Leah: she doesn't need to be told twice. She rips the Lego's cardboard. Three bags crinkle onto the table. She pops the largest, most orange one. Lester says she's meat to him if she loses a single piece.

"Are you gramps or grandpa?" Leah snaps a black one-by-two on an orange plank. "Papa Les?"

"Why in the Christ are you here?"

Pegs opens her phone. She calls up Anna's dot in Dots. The plan had been strength in numbers. The plan had also been to do some surge driving. More planning seems unwise, as does more waiting. Les and Leah are on the verge. They practically take their mail and meals on the verge. Leah tells him to hand her the windshield part of the

Lego, Lester tells her to use the Lego instructions or leave, and Pegs tells them both to be quiet. More specifically: shut up. She sticks to a single sentence: "It got changed so that the next time we wreck, you're the tow that gets the call."

No pins fall. Then, balls thump their lanes. Pins cluck off into darkness. Lester sits there like he's getting a software upgrade on the whole thing. Finally, he says: "Not a Chinaman's chance."

"Revo would pay you out for the tow job." Pegs bites the shoes off a Pilgrim cookie. "We'd sell you whatever I can squeeze from it."

"A two-fer," Leah says.

"Do they have my tax returns?" Lester asks.

Pegs makes a joke of it—they have your returns, your social, shoe size, brand of toothpaste. For all she knows, Revo does have Lester's tax returns. Her level of inquiry with Leah was low, her logistical planning lower. She hasn't thought seriously about workspace. She hasn't considered whether the car might be too damaged to move. She herself, as a driver, might be too damaged to strip it for parts. She hasn't thought past Lester saying no, which he does, again: "I don't care if they fill it with gold nickels," he tells her. "No."

Leah bails on the Lego diver. She focuses her attention on Lester. "A whole car," Leah tells him, "is a lot of parts."

"Used," Lester says.

"It's just us," Pegs says. "We'll keep it small, how it's been."

"We're reliable," Leah adds. Lester's claws return, just a bit. He doesn't blink or move, sip or breathe. He tells Leah: "You've never been in the deep end."

Leah reminds Lester that they've been swapping parts

for months. Lester says sure, he's been taking wipers, but doors? Seats? VIN numbers? He sips pink lemonade. The stuff is bright enough to signal planes. He leans forward, says Leah doesn't understand anything about nothing. He readies a long speech about the nature of risk, working alone, how to survive multiple decades in the whirlpools of American commerce, god knows what. He raises his hands. The silver hairs on his forearms swirl like the wild mane on some wizard that's readying to cast a tornado on the whole bowling alley. He pushes up his glasses, says "Here's the thing," but then he tenses. His gaze shifts. A girl is running toward them. It isn't Anna. It isn't some mom from the long shoe line asking to see the manager. It isn't Lester's daughter coming to tell him that his grandson wants his Lego. It's the waitress person. She appears to be the bowling alley's lone employee, a real jack of all trades. Her red shirt is a perfect clash with the walls, a strawberry in funky raspberries. She has misinterpreted Lester's irritation.

The girl is breathless when she arrives at their table. The rag on her shoulder drips. It's the soda she cleaned off the birthday lane. There's a wet stripe down her red shoulder. In a rush she says: It's happy hour, sides half off, Counter-Cash can take their shoe order, the one at the bar can take drinks, she'll bring them right out.

Lester tells her to relax. He says they're set. He does his low wave thing, where he opens his hand like he's dropping a mic. You're left to gauge whether he means *Thanks* or *Get lost* or *You're welcome* or *Kiss the ring*, all without ever seeing his palm.

Leah twists in her seat. It's not a graceful pivot, what with the sling. "You want some help?" she asks.

"You're sweet," the girl says.

"Dead serious." Leah stands. "I'll hand shoes."

Pegs waits for the catch—just give me a third of your tips, a tenth of your hourly. No catch comes, nor does any rebuttal from the girl. It's truly incredible how Leah gets people to go along with her. People just seem to say yes.

Pegs is one such person. Here I am, she thinks, sitting with Lester beside a rack of bowling bowls, trying to sell him on a move initiated by Leah, who stations herself at the main counter. She pulls shoes from cubbies.

"How'd she bust a wing?" Lester says.

"You could ask."

"She's dangerous." Lester grabs the Lego diver. He prances it around the table, giving it Leah's voice: "*Hey you, hey you, help me out, I help you, we all share a cell.*"

"I trust her," Pegs says.

"You don't get far with people like her," Lester says. "You wind up having to trust everyone they trust."

Pegs opens her hand, Lester-style. She has no idea what it communicates. She makes a fist and tries to set an elbow on the rack of bowling balls. There's no good angle. The pink ones on top are too high. The rack is crowded. The table is so freaking small. There's no imposing way to sit. Screw imposing. Comfort is a stretch. Her butt is still wet from the sandbags. Some thin stickiness is sealing her heavy garage shoes to the carpet. It doesn't help that Lester is sizing her up. Pegs feels like she's on the stand. It's uncomfortable. It's even weirder to feel like you're being cross-examined while the judge is blasting Bon Jovi. It feels like the judge actually is Bon Jovi, mid-song.

Lester leaves the Lego guy standing. "Loaning the tow is a no."

"It's not a loan." Pegs tells Lester that all he has to do is show up to a crash site and get the car. That's it. Literally all he has to do is take one phone call.

"Then one more, from you, in the county jail." Lester takes a cookie in his thumb and bad pointer. He pinches the turkey's feathers. He bites the head. He smacks on the gobbler like a cow going at cud. Sprinkles end up amongst the Legos. He says everyone is so desperate now, so crazy, boisterous. Up to his nose hairs: that's what Les says about his stress. The neighbors won't quit writing the council-woman about people doing drop-offs after quiet hours. Customers need turn-arounds between surges. Legos.

A family returns shoes to Leah. She stacks them like a red-brick chimney around the CounterCash.

"Leave a torch and impact wrench in the tow for me," Pegs says.

"I'll leave nothing nowhere." Lester pushes the lemonade aside. He seems ready to clear the Legos off, too. He wants a straight-ahead look at Pegs. He looks ready to level with her, to yell, to ask why she's pushing, pushing, pushing rather than just coasting, working the margins, staying sly. The DJ isn't helping. He's raising the pressure. On everything. He's so loud. The guy or robotized pro-gram or whatever is for some reason twice the volume of the techno beat. He's wishing a very special birthday to a name that Anna shouts over: "Does Leah work here?"

Anna sits in Leah's seat. She says she's sorry she's late—traffic, parking. She asks for a summary of the conversation to-date. Lester's assessment: lemonade's four bucks, Leah's a cobbler, he's blocking all nine numbers from Revo.

"I do have questions." Anna wiggles out of her rain jacket. She opens the directions for the Legos. "Are we trying to crash, or are we just crossing our fingers?"

"Your average person prays for the lotto," Lester says. "For sunshine."

Anna sifts through Legos. She finds the propeller. "An active pursuit of a vehicle complicates our incentivization in ways that require us to at least—"

"Later," Pegs says.

Lester tips his drink at Anna. It's like he's trying to squirt lemonade over her head. "You and her need to get together on this," he tells Pegs. "Then we'll talk."

Pegs says: We're talking now, we're ready. Anna says: All I got was a text! She says she's definitely, genuinely, absolutely sick over the idea of intentionally wrecking a prototype. An accident? She can deal. But she keeps coming back to incentives. They're opening up a whole new world of behaviors by offering up a benefit for a crash. It is at this Guns-n-Roses juncture that Anna directs the conversation even further away from squeezing a simple yes out of Lester. She asks: "What's even the actual cost-benefit of getting a car?"

"The cost is getting caught," Lester says.

"But what's the take?" Anna snaps a mechanical arm onto the body. The scuba-diver thing actually now looks like a scuba-diver thing. "Seems relevant."

Pegs leans back. She hides her eyes down a lane. It would be nice if the mechanical pin gatherer lifted her, whisked her around the surge-less building, and let her come back inside with a new approach.

She pictures a RedGill—where's it most likely to get hit? Which parts would be unusable? Sure, fenders have value, but they're easily injured. Most of the wheels, tires, and rims would still be salvageable. She sees the number 10,000 in her head. She ticks off parts in the engine and tries to see 15,000. She pictures Leah and Anna seeing fifteen on a sheet of paper then being told, I dunno: seven.

Lester sets down his phone. He rewinds to some pointless moment in the conversation. "I'm not closing for a day so you can run a chop shop."

"I swear on my parents I'll strip it somewhere else," Pegs says.

Anna situates the diver in its diving vehicle. "I'd like a number," she says.

"Is there really some cut off where you'll chicken out?" Pegs says.

"Why do you equate preparation with cowardice?" Anna says.

Pegs says it's guesswork, that she doesn't want to get anyone too excited. She leans toward Anna. She says stripping a prototype that's in decent enough shape can get them each a few thousand bucks. It'd be slow money—weeks, if not months. She adds: I think. Anna says: Thank you.

"I really just do not get it," Lester says. He says he'll never in all his life understand why young women would be so desperate for cash. No kids, no houses—what do they have to worry about, really?

"Loans," is all Anna says.

Lester sips. "Lend money, you buy an enemy."

"She's fifty times you," Pegs tells him. "In everything."

"At least she's got an answer."

There's clapping. It's coming from more than a single lane. The synchronized applause is being directed at Lester's grandson, who is controlling the AI soaker soldier. The kid has evidently converted it to manual. The thing is squirting a bowling ball all the way down the glossy mess of a lane. The neon orange ball is halfway to the pins.

The birthday kids are clapping in unison. The parents, too. Even Anna claps. A human DJ would spin the music low to amplify the noise created by human bones and skin, but it doesn't really matter. The crowd is louder than the music.

When the orange ball gets two thirds of the way home, it veers. The crowd gasps. Instructions are yelled: *March the soldier forward! Refill the supply line!*

It's too late. The AI soldier with swollen circular eyes runs out of fluid. Its sprayer dies. The ball rolls into the far gutter. The crowd emits a gleefully mournful noise, then decides polite applause is required. The boy gives a twitchy smile. Lester's daughter says no one can bowl until the lane is dried, but no further bowling balls head down Lane 11. No balls go down Lanes 1-10 or 12-22. Every phone in the facility chirps like a steel rooster.

Pegs can't recall ever being in such a crowded environment for a Shelter Alert. The reaction isn't panic. It's more like a six a.m. alarm. The kids are unresponsive. The parents pack up, gesture, grab items and also arms. None of them have cars that will perform well in a surge. Pegs does. She also has a co-pilot with a week left in a sling who is plugging shoes in holes as fast as she can. To free up space, Leah slides incoming shoes off the counter into the cashier's alley. She gives up on assortment of any kind. She makes a game of it, telling people they can aim for a slot, any slot.

Lester gives Pegs and Anna his low open-handed wave, says he'll think about the thing. Pegs says he's already listed as the tow, it'll be fishy if they change it. He says they'll talk. He hands the scuba to his grandson, then disappears into the crowd.

Anna zips her jacket. "Five more surge hours, double-bonus."

"So you're in?"

"I'm nervous." She stuffs the instructions in the Lego Box. She drops the box in the tall trash behind Pegs. "But I'm always nervous."

The crowd is mostly dispersed when Anna leaves. Leah and Pegs are soon the only ones left. Leah is stuffing shoes in holes at a rate that suggests she's got nowhere better to be. Pegs eats sprinkles off the table, attempting to realign her night. Two GreenGills need their brake calipers lubricated. She should drive. She should perhaps drive to Lester's to work on him alone.

She walks to the counter. Leah is hidden, on her knees. Shoes are scattered around the CounterCash, which lords over the empty lanes. Its red eyes pulse lightly, quickly. They're blinking. The rush of shoes has short-circuited it. It's like it's having a nightmare.

The shoes appear to have short-circuited more than just the CounterCash. Multiple sources of light are malfunctioning. A white light around the corner is on the fritz. Some bulb is flashing over by the bar. The pulse is erratic. It's a lighthouse beacon screaming *Reroute*.

Pegs peeks around the corner. The bulb in question is flashing from inside the dim supply closet. The waitress girl is sitting on a folding chair, eating a sandwich out of tin foil. The umbrellas and shop vac look older than her. There's a cash register, an actual metal piece of machinery. Rounded typewriter buttons bloom off the body like short flowers off a grave. Cleaners and polishers weigh the higher wooden shelves, and across from them, on the floor, a sleeping bag is kinked up on a twin mattress. The girl's smart watch brightens the supply room. It flashes at a rate that quickens Pegs' pulse.

"I can clean the soda off that lane," Pegs says. She's surprised she says it. The girl chews, shakes no.

"It's nothing," Pegs says. "I can't leave until my friend is done."

The girl's wrist blinks wildly. She doesn't seem to register it. "I'm not supposed to let anyone stay."

"It's really nothing."

"We're liable or something." She sets her sandwich on the shop vac. She stands, smooths her uniform. "I'll lock up."

12

DEATH DIRECTIONS

SURGES HAVE a way of making everyone cave. They
wear people down. Their grudges erode when daily logis-
tics and even survival become such a drag. For instance:
Pegs fully and officially caves on the idea of moving anywhere—by December first, by the end of surge season, in
her lifetime. She deletes the premium level of Rūm, also
the standard one, the works. She stops logging apartment
signs on test drives. Even if they found a place, finding a
clear day to move? Forget it. Her sister's demand: moving
and saving can't just be an idea come fall.

Lester caves on the tow. How? Via text. Why? "I wasn't
handing her a victory there." *Her* meaning Leah, *there*
meaning the bowling alley. Over five more texts, though,
she senses Lester's real reason for caving: cash. His usual
customers have not been driving. They and their cars have
been at home, sheltering. He's getting crushed. He needs
any potential revenue stream he can find.

Anna caves on her concerns re: intentionally crashing
a prototype. Pegs comes to understand that for Anna,
stealing parts was an easy proposition. There was justice
to it—the drivers were taking pieces of technology that

weren't in use; the drivers then transported these parts to a location where the items could fulfill their technological destiny. The setup worked for someone like Anna, whose technological know-how and enthusiasm, though dampened by several hundred driving shifts at Revo, taught her that making technological processes more efficient is a net positive. Intentionally damaging a groundbreaking prototype is a harder sell to someone like Anna. Destruction is not in her DNA. Multiple texts from Anna begin with *I'm having a hard time...*, but again: surges, student loans, so on, and she caves. God bless grad school.

Leah, of course, doesn't cave on a single thing. Leah constructs elaborate new subterranean caverns for people to cave into. She's relentless in the group chat. She brainstorms what becomes a rolling manual of best practices for when, where, and how to unsuspiciously wreck a driverless prototype while on a company-monitored automated test drive. Pegs starts to think of them as the Death Directions. They're perhaps a bit on the safe side, but they aren't bad. Leah's idea is to make better use of Pittsburgh's insane topography, which has played a small but significant role in the city becoming the capital of the driverless-car world across the twenty-first century. The landscape poses built-in challenges for all of the AV companies, and built-in means free. There's heat, there's snow, and there are surges. There are tunnels and potholes. What feels like half the region's school districts are '[Insert] Hills.' It may soon be more than half; many municipalities are petitioning for hill-related name changes to ensure that their real estate sounds higher and thus better equipped to handle surge season. Toss in 446 bridges that cross three major rivers, plus ninety hyper-distinct neighborhoods that are often topographically walled off from one another, and what you wind up with is a road system that is total disorder. The place is a right angle's nightmare. It's pavement laid on earthen chaos. Roads rise and bank, span river valleys and mountains, contort themselves across wet and wild unruly terrain.

It's honestly a miracle they haven't wrecked a prototype every day.

Leah's first Death Direction concerns slopes. She tells Pegs and Anna to target roads where the run-off might be especially severe during a surge. Leah's thinking is that the steeper the road, the harder an object might slide down into the hood. Pegs waits for a surge, then she sees how BlueGill1 does on Rialto Street and its twenty-five percent grade. Rain cannonballs into the hood. Sticks, too. The tires feel square-like. She can picture it: BG1 being hit, rolling backward, forty-million miles down, then: impact. Lester gets the call. Pegs gets some sort of whiplash, time off. More importantly, she gets a discarded car she can pick clean as a carcass.

None of this happens. The BlueGill delivers her to the top of Troy Hill with barely a change in speed.

13

NEW PLAN

COBBLESTONES! Leah advises Pegs and Anna to spend as many driving hours as possible looping Oakland. Specifically, she tells them to go down steep Chesterfield, over and over. The cobblestones punch the intelli-grip tires, though it turns out that the bigger threat is posed by Oakland's many college students. More specifically, by how sloppy Pitt students are with their possessions. Cars are badly parked. Someone has failed to pick up a couch that is now soaked. It's sitting where a car should be. Trash bags roll and split because apparently students are too cheap to have trash barrels, though it's possible landlords are too cheap to provide them.

The place is paradise for the disorderly and destructive. Pegs is confident they'll get their first car in Oakland. In a daytime surge on a Tuesday, she can see the specific cobblestone on Chesterfield that will do the trick. The gray block rises off the street like a thumbs-up.

The RedGill avoids it. It avoids the angularly parked Subaru, too. Pegs is dropped down onto Fifth Avenue just fine. On the loop back toward Cardiac Hill, all of the high dorm windows are bright. The students are inside the Towers, bored, sheltering, nowhere to go. Pegs thinks she can see two heads, up high, tracking her. The bastards don't know how good they have it, though they're probably saying the same.

14

O . B . Z . C .

IT'S SO OBVIOUS: if the goal is neglected or
dangerous infrastructure, where better than a Black neighborhood? Leah makes a whole big fuss to Dellinger about
how their test drives pass through predominately white
spaces, ten to one, easy. She says Revo needs to ensure that
all neighborhoods are equally mapped. Dellinger shares
map data that indicates everywhere is quite mapped and
driven, thank you. Leah threatens to go higher.

Thus Operation Black Zip Code is born. Leah's math
on the increased risk profile is fuzzier than Lester's forearms. She's always texting long reports and then claiming
that it's like, half a percentage point more likely that a
falling phone wire garrots them in a Black neighborhood.
She crunches numbers on a decade of paving schedules.
Her argument, heavily disputed by Anna: they're five to
seven percent more likely to experience a wreck on a Black
street than on a white one.

The problem is that the prototypes seem to know the
math better than Leah.

Take Homewood, late Thursday afternoon. Bad surge
coming, out of nowhere, any second. The fastest route—

the one that RedGill3 has already outlined—is to hang a right down Tioga Street.

But the RedGill hesitates. It calculates. Maybe it senses an airborne threat being whisked along by hard winds. The telepoles and wires on Tioga do look suspect. They shake. The poles lack traffic sensors, as do most public surfaces in Homewood, and Pegs wonders: is the car changing routes because the system is worried about old telepoles?

Or: is the system concerned because it can't find another technological object to communicate with?

And what about the boys? Does the presence of Black boys scare off the RedGill? Two, then as many as five Black kids run out into the darkening yards. They pick up footballs and plastic toddler toys that are shaking in the emergent wind. The boys carry bikes onto porches, then indoors. One boy is a girl, tall and strong, and Pegs wonders if the prototype is now heading straight instead of right as a way to avoid these children. She wonders if the mothers on the porches waving children inside have witnessed the fancy car consider them then reroute. Pegs can't gauge their expressions in the rearview mirror. She turns backward, fully. She wants a better look. She wants to know: did the car reroute because of incoming weather or current people? Was it infrastructure? What's it scared of? She'd like to know so she can guide the prototype more regularly toward what it fears. Maybe it's scared of the pebbles filling all the potholes. Wind-blown weeds cut like lightning across the street, then they're flattened by rain.

The car chirps. It halts. Pegs braces her shoulders. She ducks her head between the seats, anticipating an airborne threat—falling drone, telepole, who knows. Rain pounds the hood, windshield, and roof. Something heavier is on the way. She reaches for her pocket, her phone. She'll warn Lester—call coming, remember the torch. She'll text the drivers—I'm fine.

Nothing lands. She breathes. She faces fully forward. The console screen blinks redly:

DISENGAGED—INATTENTIVE.

15

BRAKE-PAD BIBLE

NO ONE AT REVO cares about her Inattentive in Homewood. There's no mention of a re-train. There's not even a call about it. Those staffed at Revo on Thursday afternoon only care that the car performed well in the surge—and surges have become increasingly dangerous. The oldest tree in the county, a tall five-hundred-year-old oak, gets plucked from the earth. There are multiple stories about how the three rivers are climbing the barrier at Point State Park, the concrete of which has been raised, but evidently not enough. Sewers erupt in five separate neighborhoods. It's as though the surges are a hard pointy hammer rapping on every bone in the city's skeleton.

But the surges won't tap on the cars. Not hard enough, at least. The surges don't create the right kind of danger. They create a kind of continual, low-grade panic that never quite delivers an outcome the drivers can benefit from.

Namely, an embarrassingly wrecked car that Revo is eager to covertly dispose of without a care for where it winds up.

Nothing they try works. The infrastructure plays always look so good—crumbling tunnels, wobbly telepoles, old overflowing bridges without downspouts—but it's impossible to time the moment of their failure. Operation Alley dings some fenders. All it means is more work for Pegs in the garage. The driver monitoring system is impossible to trick. Pegs tries to pantomime fear into the dash, flashing her teeth in a panicked grimace. The system doesn't bite, swerve, stop, anything. It doesn't assume an incoming foe. There's an incoming call about it, a rarity. It's Argentau, from Ops: "I'm not a dentist."

Whenever the surges relent, Pegs makes a habit of finding the surge-pay protesters. She instructs the prototype to loop the block, hoping the protesters might throw something. They never do. They pose no real threat to her two-ton mobile fortress. They raise flimsy signs, all of which are weighed by rain and time. The nuns have traded in their habits for snow hats and rubber boots, like they're waiting for sled dogs to whisk them to a drier jurisdiction.

She sees Leah with the protesters only once. Pegs doesn't need the skeleton mask or red rain boots to know it's her. She knows it's Leah because of how Leah approaches the first car that the protesters stop. Leah leans down to the driver. She touches her own knees but not the man's Kia. She's right in his window, three cars ahead of Pegs' GreenGill, but Leah's not being pushy about it. In fact, she's so unpushy that she quickly decides she's not the right person for the job, and waves over a separate protester to talk to the driver. It's clear Leah has determined, in under twenty seconds, who the driver is, what matters to them, and which protester is best equipped to convince this driver that society needs a massive overhaul in how it pays people and keeps them safe.

It really is incredible to watch. Leah makes such quick,

confident decisions in the presence of strangers. Pegs wonders: how long would it take *her* to become comfortable ap-
proaching cars and talking to drivers? Once comfortable,
it would take an additional number of months or years to
actually be effective at it. She doubts she'd ever acquire the
wherewithal to call over a friend—to have devoted all that
time to improving her ability to talk, and then to hand
the mic to someone else. Pegs doesn't even know what to
call this special superpower of Leah's. It's not quite se-
duction. It's more earnest than that. Pegs can't recall ever
feeling tricked by Leah. She's been bulldozed. She's been
ignored. But she wouldn't say she's been tricked. The communication is always very clear, if at times delayed. Pegs
watches Leah walk to the second car in line, and when another protester comes to ask Leah a question, Leah blows
her off while she leans down to the driver. This, it strikes
Pegs, is why Leah's communication is sometimes delayed
or frustrating—she's always focusing on the next person.
Once you're on her team, she knows she has you, and only
addresses you directly when she decides she can enlist you
in the effort to secure that *next* person.

What the drivers cannot secure is a car. They fail to do
so, shift after shift, day after day. It all feels like such a
letdown. It feels as though the three test drivers agreed to
step over this invisible barrier together into a new world
of risk, yet for ten days, nothing has changed.

Ten days, no crash.

Ten days, a few measly payouts from Lester for parts
they dropped off weeks ago.

Ten days, and Pegs can never coordinate her schedule to
earn a surge bonus.

Ten days, each of them a failure. Anna texts whenever a Death Direction is unsuccessful. Leah tells her that ideas are free, she could provide her own, live dangerously, brainstorm badly. It's a constant, endless, annoying back and forth: Anna says the ideas aren't working because the risk percentages are too small, Leah says let's get riskier, Anna says um no are you insane, Leah says you can either castigate or participate, or some slogany thing.

Pegs is at a red light when Anna approaches, across the intersection. Anna's BlueGill brakes thoughtfully at the light, patiently, environmentally, as though it's looking both ways to make sure no insects are harmed in the termination of its velocity. The four blue slashes on its gray door stand for computing, the environment, and...innovation? Safety? Pegs can never remember them all. What she thinks is: the most profitable solution would be simply driving straight into Anna. They'd wind up with two damaged cars. The issue: Pegs would get fired. She'd lose her garage salary. Her driver's rate, too.

It's all so complex. They have to maximize their secret profit while retaining employment and also keeping everyone—themselves, the public—safe. There are so many constraints to work around, perhaps too many. It's a lot to ask of three overworked women. Lester's contributions are minimal. He never texts to ask if they're safe. His texts only reiterate that he's not towing a damaged prototype to his garage. The next text says he forwarded money—shock absorbers. He wants Pegs to check it to make sure it went through. *This crypto shit*, he writes, and then there's an emoji of a dog. Then a gun. He says he meant the gun. Ignore the dog.

Pegs misses doing drop-offs at Lester's. She misses the pre-surge era when the garage was quiet, when the drivers could load parts into trunks, unsurveilled. Now, the drivers are rarely even together. When Tuesday evening's shelter alert hits, Anna takes GreenGill3 out into a light surge, Leah chases her in a RedGill, and once Door 2 closes, Pegs is trapped inside the garage with cars, work stations, and computer people. It's as though she's trapped in a maze. She has been transferred inside the PacMan arcade game that the CEO keeps in his office, except these ghosts don't chase her. These ghosts sit at makeshift work stations that are jammed between prototypes, blocking the way.

She lifts the small rolly floor jack over the wires and cords running to Argentau's standing desk. He's beside a GreenGill and looks like he's about to speak to her, except he's just kind of speaking to himself, it seems. When the guy thinks, it's like he's communicating telepathically with someone in a purple-hued future dimension, which is how Smith from Computing Vision looks, too. The guy isn't shaving until the cars are licensed. His beard is practically stirring his smoothie. The longer parts of the beard are turning the color of saltwater foam. His facial hair is honestly nicer to look at than Bickner, who is at a cheap, cluttered folding table and who has recently made a switch to tighter, more fashionable khakis. Bickner intermittently breaks from typing to reach into his bunched-up crotch and release quickly so that no one sees, except it sort of has the opposite effect. The big flourishing release is like he's performing a middle school timpani solo and his parents are in the last row.

The men, like their vehicles, are programmed to focus on the task they've been assigned. This means they ignore Pegs. Pegs ignores them back. She tries to, anyways. It's hard. Their laptop screens and logos shine like streetlights in the polished car frames.

Pegs drops the jack at BlueGill1. She breaks the nuts
on the front left tire. The surge welting the garage doors
sounds more than light. Two cars are on routes, meaning two potential wrecks. A surge also means surge hours.
She's in the realm of a surge bonus. It's a long shot, but
it's possible, and she tells herself: finish this, then drive;
control what you can. She jacks up the frame. She removes
the tire and slides it beneath the BlueGill.

Boltz and Stomanovich get up from their chairs. They
do a lap. They're like drunk hunters, disturbing the environment, pointing their instruments at irresponsible
angles. Pegs assumes they'll pass her, but when she finishes breaking the calipers, the two brown-haired guys are
standing right behind her. The shorter Boltz is rotating an
apple-sized gyroscope, which Pegs tends to define as "if
an eyeball had a skeleton." He pets its gimbals and rotors
playfully, like he's plucking petals: *It loves me, it's just a bot.*

Pegs points her socket wrench. "Toy problems?"

"In graduate school," Boltz informs her, "I used these to
help send a Rover to Mars."

Pegs zip-ties the caliper to the strut. She doesn't tell
Boltz that exploring Mars might have been a more pro-
ductive response to climate change than spending a decade
cycling through business models for driverless cars. The
taller Stomanovich offers her his extra protein squeezer,
from the caf. It's a pink tube whose contents most closely
resemble pinto beans eaten by a hairy pig then shat out,
voila.

Before she can decline, all three of them are startled by
a crash outside the garage. No other impact follows. The
three of them relax.

Boltz asks about the zip tie, the caliper. Why can't she
just set whatever it is on the workbench?

"It's connected to the brake fluid line," Pegs says.

"Why's the tire beneath the car?" Boltz asks.

The tire is there in case the jack fails, though if the surge gets any louder, it might be thunder that shakes the car onto Pegs. It sounds wicked out. She checks her phone—nothing from Leah or Anna. Their dots are dotting around in Dots. She asks again what the two guys want. The kinder Stomanovich whacks the protein squeezer against his palm. He takes the lead:

"We were wondering if we could bring the ping-pong table down."

Pegs wiggles out the old brake pad. She wants to say: what is it with you people and ping-pong? Why not something less clunky, like darts? Or cards? Long river walks along the sandbags?

"Aren't you guys slammed?" she says.

Stomanovich shrugs. "Everyone's waiting on Prediction and Vision."

"We wouldn't be waiting," Boltz says, "if they installed a less risk-averse profile."

"It's my risk," Pegs says.

Stomanovich counters that it's everybody's risk; if the cars aren't confident enough to combat the weather, the company will stop existing. Pegs says that if the cars get too confident, it'll be her that stops existing. Surprisingly, the itchy-seeming Boltz takes her side. He steps closer, says Pegs is smart to be skeptical. He shields her from whoever is in the nearest chair—Smith, Argentau, she can't tell. It's like Boltz is about to press a button on the gyroscope that flicks out a knife, and he'll stab her and shove her underneath the raised car. She grips the socket wrench tightly.

"We actually want to talk to you about something," Boltz says.

"Discreetly," Stomanovich says.

Pegs opens the box of brake pads. She coats the top pad with her nervous breath. "Not ping-pong?"

Neither man laughs. Neither speaks. Pegs futzes with the brake pad. There's not much to futz with. She counsels herself to look down. She doesn't know what her eyes or soul might reveal if she looks up. Nerves? Guilt? She can't see whether the door to the supply room is open. There's a GreenGill in the way.

Finally, Boltz speaks: "Pick one: Wheel or Trav."

Pegs asks him to repeat the question. Boltz explains that Wheel and Trav are names. Wheel, Boltz says, is the world's original technology. Stomanovich argues that Trav actually has AV in the name.

"Is somebody pregnant or something?" Pegs says.

"We're brainstorming," Boltz says. "A company."

Pegs turns toward them. She stays on the ground. She wags the socket wrench. "Couple of secret agents," she says.

Stomanovich moves protein around the pink tube. "You of all people know that the hardware angle isn't worth it."

Pegs removes a brake pad from the box. She's unsure what "isn't worth it" about Revo's hardware or why she's supposed to know this. She taps the wrench on her thigh.

"We know you've got background," Stomanovich says. "Robotics."

Pegs keeps her face still. She taps the BlueGill with her fingers. "Just these," she says.

"The money's not in hardware," Boltz says. "That's obvious."

"Right." Pegs doesn't know what is obvious or right. She doesn't know how to ask for clarification without sounding like some idiot version of her mother.

"There's no profit humping cars." Boltz winds up his stubby little foot to kick the BlueGill. Pegs whacks his shin with the socket wrench. He yelps. She points at the car, the jack, says, "Easy. What do you want?"

Boltz and Stomanovich trip over each other explaining their idea. They do so via incomprehensibly technical descriptions. Their whole business angle has to do with the manufacturing of lidar eyes or some such thing on infrastructure items, and also satellites, maybe planes. The airborne devices will communicate with cars about airborne threats. When Pegs asks how it's any different than the traffic sensors on telepoles, the men reiterate that they're tired of working with cars directly. Boltz squeezes his gyroscope and claims they can scrape seed money for a venture without violating the direct components of their non-competes. Stomanovich outlines the company flow chart, emphasizing that with a large enough team well-versed in—

The language gets so technical. The men make no effort at translation. Concepts and terms pour from their mouths. Then, when they use the word *optoelectronics*, it hits her: they think she's Anna.

Pegs nods at them, open-mouthed. Her first thought is to text her sister: *People here think I'm smart enough to have a graduate degree.* Her second thought is to text Leah and Anna on their drives: *Misinformed enthusiasm—the Revo way!!!* It's genuinely stunning to see two people be so excited and so wrong, although the more they talk, the more it seems that it's not a simple Anna-for-Pegs mixup.

Boltz and Stomanvich seem to think there is some magical woman at Revo who is a mechanic and has a graduate degree and is also Leah, too. They're pulling in elements of all three.

Pegs spaces out on somewhere between ten and ninety percent of the pitch. She tells them it's a solid idea but that, at the moment, she's behind. She tells them she's got to keep up appearances, right? She authorizes them to bring down the ping-pong table, she'll play with them, hear them out, relax a bit. She can't actually authorize a ping-pong table, but she knows Stomanovich and Boltz probably aren't bold enough to actually walk up to the second floor and move it down to the garage themselves. The same goes for their company, Wheel or Trav or whatever. They're pretty typical Revo guys in this regard: they want big risky changes, but they don't want to be the ones to actually press the button. They want deniability of some kind—*The mechanic roboticist girl said we could bring the table down!* She watches Boltz and Stomanvich finish their lap and can easily picture their idea of a sexual fantasy: minimalist Airbnb, a Young Zuckerberg mask, coin-flipping app.

On the other side of the coin: it would have cost her nothing to be more enthusiastic about their interest. Their interest was in her. So what if it was misinformed? It was an opportunity. It was conversation. Half the men in the garage probably ascended to their stock-optioned station in life by lying in small but significant ways. She should've outlined her skills. There's plenty she can do that no one else at Revo can match. Instead, she nodded. She pretended to be someone else. She sat there blinking in a crouch.

She looks at her seated outline in the car's gray reflection.

It's the same pose as the waitress in the bowling alley who sat in a closet eating a sandwich beside a sleeping bag.

The storm taps Door 1 or 2. There's a deep rumble. It peters out. The air goes out of her at the thought of being no different than the girl in the bowling alley—a zombie blind to the signals the world is sending. She left Lester's to earn more financial stability at Revo. She said yes to driving for the same reason. She started moving parts out of trunks because she was still living in a basement, and when she aligns these individual choices into a daisy chain of continually inadequate cashflow, it panics her. Her temples sweat. She exhales. Inhaling feels hard, like it might hurt.

She tries to think of decisive, life-changing actions she can institute, right now.

Join up with Boltz and Stomanovich? There's nothing to join.

Steal more from Revo? Ten days, nothing.

She squeezes the old brake pad in her hand. It's flat, worn, a step stone in a river rising every hour. The wear on the face is like a cave drawing done with a penny. She scans it closely for some message that says: *Reinsert me into BlueGill1*. It strikes her as the most powerful decision she can make. She could intentionally sabotage a prototype. She could accept bodily risk for financial gain.

She scans the garage. If she kept a dodgy brake pad in BlueGill1, Boltz and Stomanovich would never know. Boltz is showing his gyroscope to Bickner, who doesn't care. Stomanovich is back at his station. He's got the Revo stare going—mouth open, bottom eyelids dragged down by invisible fingertips. Dellinger, Yabner, Argentau—the only autopsies they perform are on the systems, not the cars, which they ditch before anyone can take a look. Leah and Anna don't know anything about brake pads. Then, in a day, or a week, or a month, the prototype would skid, hit a pole, oops. That's why there are airbags, inflatable seat belts. What gives her pause isn't that someone would get hurt. It's that it would reflect poorly on her work.

Feet approach. Pegs shoves the old brake pad back into the slot. She removes it. She hides it behind her knee. A low shadow oozes along the aisle between the gray cars. Some employee has been on all fours, listening, spying. The feet crawl past a tire.

It's a coffee cone. It rolls slowly, as though on a check-out belt. There's no coffee in the cranial holsters. Pegs leans, hungry. She opens the chest. Trash spills out. Two cups leak brown rivers across the garage. A water bottle empties part of itself across the concrete toward Pegs' knee. There's no food.

She doesn't clean the spill. She won't. She refuses. She thinks of laying the old brake pad on the spill, as some kind of unintelligible protest, but the thing about the brake pad is: it isn't even all that bad. It's totally fine for a normal car. What's not fine is the choices she faces, every day. They're so lame.

Clean someone else's crap or leave a mess.

Work tirelessly without gain or sabotage dangerously on the margins for a mostly insignificant boost.

What she wants is impossible. She wants a tidy form of chaos that causes nobody any real problems. She wants to retain her blue-collar mantra of hard work and reliability, the safety of her body and her friends' bodies, while also acquiring more money, a higher apartment, and oh yeah, it'd be fun to stick it to a company where the men don't

know her name, except the company can't really be aware
that Pegs is sticking it to them; the company has to keep
sending her hourly payments, in perpetuity. It's a tidy kind
of destruction that feels unrealistic. It feels childlike, un-
real, a storyline from the fantasy stuff Avery reads while
sheltering. It's actually worse than that—it's downright
dictatorial to orchestrate events in your favor without any
cost or risk to you.

She tells herself to act more like a rebel, a visionary.
Burn stuff! Threaten someone! The surge outside the
doors can apparently see this thought of hers. It shudders.
More likely, it laughs. She considers the old brake pad in
her hands. She tries again to read its scratches and wear
for some kind of message. She looks at its reflection in the
gray car door. It looks like she's holding a black bible that
doesn't open.

"Whoa," Dellinger says.

Some invisible switch is thrown in the garage. The lap-
toppers activate. It's as though a secret bonus opp has been
emailed out: if the ten disparate men can finish their task
in the next thirty seconds, they'll receive their very own
smoothie machine plus free install in their eighth-floor
loft. Crosstalk fires off like impact wrenches. Dellinger
types like he's pressing his space bar ten thousand times.
Bickner stands, tugs his khakis down his thighs, and departs. He returns to the workbench for his laptop. Smith
runs to Dellinger's station so fast he doesn't realize his
beard has contacted his smoothie.

Yabner yells. "Check this out."

Pegs joins the gathering behind him. He shows the group
a still frame from a driver monitoring system. It's Anna, in
a GreenGill. Her eyes are in the middle of shrinking from

wide to shut. Her hands flail. The seat belt has inflated. An airbag bursts from the bottom of the screen like a white fist. Her mouth is contorted in a scream.

PART III
Thanksgiving Eve

16

LOGISTICAL NIGHTMARES, PLURAL

LESTER'S TOW may as well be a cement mixer. It's got no get-up, no rev. The acceleration is slushy and then some. The turn radius is nimble as a treadmill. Pegs tells herself: you are very long now; drive long, drive slow.

The first right turn is a disaster. She vacations in the opposite lane, then straightens too quickly. The impact wrench and torch crash to the floor on the passenger's side. Pegs glances in the side mirror. She half expects to see Lester chasing her through the rain in his stupid wide-brimmed hat—*Don't lose my tools, I need the tow back by Wednesday.* All she sees in the mirror is the dark outline of Anna's GreenGill, concealed in black wrap like an evil present. The car scoots into the correct lane, behind the tow.

She stays in every right lane that's offered. She briefly forgets how to find the windshield wipers, then finds them, ups them. Twice, she drops her hands off the wheel. She raises them quickly. Her feet feel heavy, stiff. She has to remember to actually, you know, drive, stay awake, be a human, respect the road. She swears there's a six-wheeler from Ryde on every block. They're like blind Dobermans

with weird cones on their roofs, prowling, trying—ineffectually—to scare rain from the city. The surge is constant.
It's more of a rain surge than a wind surge. The bridge
gutters up ahead pour like taps. The asphalt experiences
several thousand watery collisions per second, and that's
just what she can see. She can feel each drop on the tow,
on the blackly wrapped GreenGill. She tells herself: drive
like a hearse.

The nice thing about the Liberty Bridge, though, is that
there's not much for the surge to throw at her. There are
no addresses, no residences. No trash cans, benches. An
empty surging bridge is a safe place, all things considered.
Nothing bigger than a raindrop hits the tow's massive
windshield. Nothing flies past. She knows there's water
far down on either side of her, but it's not as though the
surge can lift it. Human junk is the dangerous stuff. There's
none. The one renegade drone clings to an overhead lane
signal.

The cell towers high up on Mount Washington argue in
clear red beeps, and she exits the bridge to join them. The
road steepens. She cuts the rain with wiper fluid, just to
see if it helps. The tow can't break twenty-five up the hill.
It can't hit third. *Come on, let's go*—each encouragement
does little.

As they crest onto Mount Washington, downtown becomes a low distant portrait. It's hard to see the city in full.
Between the high dark rivers and the thick surge, the skyscrapers seem shrunken, as though the've been beheaded
and be-legged. Point State Park doesn't look like a leafy
park at the confluence of the three rivers. It's a black trian-
gular vortex where the skyscrapers disappear.

Everyone has disappeared in Duquesne Heights, too.

They're hiding from the surge. Pegs tries not to use the gas. It's difficult, what with the various slopes. She wants to drive invisibly. The tow is so loud, the neighborhood so nebby. Pegs keeps thinking she'll see some curious head appear in a window, but most windows are boarded. All the plywood must be killing the local gossip. In the neighborhood next door, Mount Washington, there are scenic rivers and skyscrapers to peer down at, but in Duquesne Heights, her mother often says, people just look down at each other. They'll bitch and moan for days after hearing a single Spanish syllable being uttered on the worksite for the tall million-dollar condo, the one with rare views of Point State Park. They'll post in four separate online forums if they find the grass too shaggy on the sloping vacant lot, the one that's been listed at 30k for three years. If it wasn't surging, the O'Neill's would definitely stop the tow and ask what happened to the car, whose is it, what's the story. The Jacksons would call the cops. The Oljuski's are themselves cops. The plywood at the McGarrity's tough metal-looking little cottage is poorly applied. The wood is tilted if you look closely, which of course Pegs, as a daughter of Duquesne Heights, does. No one is peeking out of the dark gaps in the corners.

She backs Anna's wrapped prototype and then the tow down her parents' sloped driveway. She opens the driver's door into rain. Water pools at the base of the slope, half a foot of it. Sandbags are lined in front of the garage door. She kicks at the long grated drain. It's clogged only by water. There's a blank rectangle where the keypad used to be, and so she hoists the garage door open to her knees. The rest can't be done quietly. The door joggles and whines against the brown ceiling springs.

Water rushes over empty cement. It swirls at drains.
Fortunately, nothing inside the one-car garage is on the
ground. High shelves are lined with small space heaters
and old paint. Kitchen chairs hang on nails that are long
enough to tunnel a brick. She kicks at a sandbag. It's firm.
As she debates whether the prototype will be able to roll
over it without an ability to accelerate, the air in the garage
changes. The flow is altered. The narrow white door to the
basement is open.

"We have phones, Jan."

Her father isn't angry. He's never angry. Like Pegs, he's
got kind eyes and a mean face. It's the mouth that does it.
The mustache, really. His gray mustache is older than him.
He and his Tyrannausauric thighs crouch to drop sandbags in the doorway to the basement. He leans into the
cold garage until he spots the tow and wrapped monstros-
ity, right there on his slope. Water steadily leaks through
the sandbags, maybe under them, too.

"Is this a *now* thing?" her father asks.

"Pretty much."

"Christmas gift?"

Pegs starts kicking the top row of sandbags to the side.
Her father helps and complains. The garage will soak, he
says. She reminds him that he owns ninety-seven shop-
vacs. He tells her to put the car in neutral, then they'll
push it over the remaining sandbags, to which she says: it's
already in neutral, I can't get inside the thing, it's wrapped,
are your contacts in? She tells him to move. She undoes
the tow's metal pins. The GreenGill departs the towing
bracket. Her hope: the grade and weight will propel the
wrapped car over the sandbags.

The reality: the GreenGill hits the sandbags and sticks

in them, horribly, tragically. The front hood and roof get
drilled by rain.

Pegs curses. She curses louder. Her jacket hood is down.
She doesn't care. Her father asks what the goal is and she
says what does it look like, we need to get the car inside.
She lifts sandbags away from where the tires hit. Together,
they clear a path. The water appreciates this. It rushes past
though not quite over her garage shoes. Her father yanks
up two cones from the cement floor like they're fossilized
beets or turnips from some dino-century, shouting some
deranged thing about emergency drainage as Pegs grabs
the kitchen chairs off hooks. She assembles them at the
back of the garage, a quick dinner party, no table, just chat.
She isn't sure it'll be enough to keep the prototype from
mashing the rear wall if it ever really gets rolling. The dryer
and washer on the side of the garage are empty. They're at-
tached to too many wires and pipes to be moved.

She steps over the sandbags in the side doorway. She
enters her childhood bedroom, in the basement. She scans
for padding. She'd like to sleep on a dry bed. Ditto pil-
low. The rest of what she sees isn't hers. It's storage. It's
crap, basically, none of it useful to her as padding. Cans
line the shelves near the stairs, their labels shiny, grimed.
How can a woman buy and forget about so many Cris-
cos? Applesauces have settled into apples and whatever
else her mother jars inside, although the cans and jars are
at least rowed. Bushels of clothes and fabrics are grouped
in low distinct clumps on Pegs' old desk. Detaching the
Pittsburgh potty would be disastrous—the lone wobbly
wall would not conceal whatever smell or creature might
emerge from the drain pipe if the standalone toilet is dis-
turbed for the first time since, oh, the Great Depression.

The exercise machine is a complete anomaly. It's downright alien. It cannot possibly have been a purchase. It is most definitely an item one of her parents said *Hm* about on trash day and then ferried home and never used. The machine appears to be an elliptical, a simple, juniorish one. It's more like a broken, headless robot. Pegs drags it out of her bedroom and into the garage. She shoves it amongst the wooden chairs protecting the rear wall.

She tells her father to stand in the doorway. She raises the tow's bracket and jumps up into the cab. She doesn't look behind her. It's easier to drive backwards when you're looking dead-straight ahead. She knows what's behind her—a prototype, the stone sidewall, washer, dryer. She gasses lightly, in reverse, just a big toe. The tow meets the GreenGill. She nestles up against it and gasses, gently. She revs to a two count, then brakes. When she jogs into the garage, the prototype is beyond the sandbags. Her father is salvaging the one chair that isn't smashed. The elliptical? Indestructible.

They recreate the sandbags at the mouth of the garage as best they can. Pegs borrows some bags from the side doorway to her bedroom. She slams the garage door while her father shop vacs. He aims a leaf blower at one of the smaller, piston-sized drains. The air blanket he lays by the threshold is even louder. It sounds like five jetliners circling a tarmac. He steps into the house with Pegs and shuts the door on all the air mechanisms in the garage. They sit on the stairs to the kitchen. Father and daughter drip, breathe.

"I left some tool bags somewhere," she says.

Her father exhales. He looks like he's drafting a police report in his head. Either that, or he's about to tell her how much he has missed doing these goofy ridiculous projects. He wipes snot or rain off his mustache. "I kind of remember them."

"They never came to my apartment."

He blows his nose in his rain-soaked red shirt. "Is that Lester's tow?"

"Who else?" she says, then stands and parts the fabrics. No tools are hidden on the table. The fresh empty space smells like the inside of an empty nail hole. "I'll park it behind you on the street."

"Is this another weird thing off the web?"

Pegs finds pliers in her desk. Little else is hers. It's shocking to see how much stuff has wound up in her room. Five or six of the deer paintings on canvas are by her grandpa, a mill worker who painted and drank instead of talking. There are a few imitations done by her dad, but his deer are rounder and hate eye contact. It's as though her room is now an ark packed with bucks and does. They're waiting to see if the nests of fabric are safe to sleep in. Pegs doesn't even know if fabric is the right word. She picks up an orange slice of the stuff and thinks: in a pinch, this could wrap a headlight. Although: the front left headlight is what dove into the pothole. It won't be sellable.

She waves the orange fabric. "Is this up for grabs?"

"She'll murder you." Her father stands. She's shocked to realize that he's dressed for his Macy's shift—khakis, red button down. It's got to be ten by now, maybe ten thirty. She asks if he's heading in.

"They're doubling surge pay if you stock this week," he says.

"It's bad out," she says. Her father replies in a mumble. His own father's deer stare at him, saying: speak up. He opens the door to the tarmac. She has to shout: "Take a jacket, you big dummy."

"They get stolen from the lounge." He checks the garage floor with the back of his palm. He says to leave the blowers on another ten, then shop-vac anywhere that shines. He points at his shoes. "Down here, water's death."

17

THE BLACK WRAP

PEGS DOES not sleep, not at first. She paces in the one-car garage. She kicks and spits at every shiny drain. The crashing was supposed to be the hard part. Getting Lester to tow the vehicle was the hard part. Getting the godforsaken prototype into her parents' sloping sandbag of a driveway was the hard part.

The hard part, it turns out, is the wrap.

She surveys the gray car, which is no longer gray. The car is wrapped in black. It's like the car dressed itself in a sexy catsuit thing for Halloween and decided to wear it clear through Thanksgiving. It's unclear whether Pegs will be able to get the stuff off by Christmas, even. It is not normal car wrap. It isn't cheap vinyl you can heat and peel. The tires are exposed, but the rest of the car hides underneath an impenetrable membrane. The rack and lidar on the roof? Gone, extracted and saved by the breakdown crew. What's left is black material hellbent on maintaining an airless relationship with the car's exterior. The stuff is like her rain jacket except thinner, and tighter, and somehow far, far nastier.

Three different screw drivers don't puncture the skin.

Midnight knives and scissors spiral like Q-tips. She can poke one arm of her father's hedge clippers through the surface, but she can't cut. There's no leverage.

Revo, she thinks, is selling the wrong product. They should get in the wrap game, the secrecy game, the "make your embarrassingly damaged products disappear" game. By her second meatloaf sandwich the next morning, she's stumped enough to call Lester, who says: I want the tow back by tonight, people drink, they drive, doesn't matter there's supposed to be a howitzer of a surge, the Wednesday before Thanksgiving means tow jobs, guaranteed. She files her PTO claim while sitting on the elliptical. In the notes field, she says she'll fill all ten road hours over the holiday. Anna struggles to text, what with her arm, so she video conferences. She wants to see the car. Pegs says it doesn't really look like a car in its current condition.

"Is that it behind you?"

"That's the dryer."

"Did you gut it?"

Pegs says: not exactly. Anna shares every exact detail of her whole traumatic crash story. Cardboard from some big appliance wound up flat across a huge pothole. The prototype dove. Anna's wrist would not have shattered if she'd been holding the wheel. Her hands had activated out of instinct.

Pegs' hands stay active as Anna talks. She texts Leah to sit tight, don't come yet, she's not ready to load a trunk. She pauses her assault on the black wrap to stare at it while seated on the washer. She lays on the dry ground and scooches underneath the frame. It's as though a black rubber organism has enveloped the car. The stuff feels alive. She pinches it, it recoils. She rubs it until it whines.

It's got a kind of fungal creativity that makes her question the people she's up against. If they can create this kind of protection to lock away their failures, they can probably lock her away, too. They can track what she's up to, follow her, hear her, see her, maybe smell her. Twice she catches herself looking at the garage door. There's no movement, no reflection. There's white paint. The drains gurgle.

Upstairs, her sister arrives to cook. Pegs shuts the door to the garage. She thinks of which part would be easiest to forfeit if she opts to simply wail away. The rear left window strikes her as a safe option. She crouches at the front bumper, which is contorted, impaled. The pothole Anna hit must've been two, three feet wide.

She hides her eyes inside goggles. She flares the torch twice. It responds. She kneels at the dent, aims and fires, holding the flame steady. Her temples sweat. The outer layer of wrap starts to think about bubbling up. Then, it smolders. The smell is as dense and tough as the material itself. She closes her eyes. Her hands stay steady. Her mom and sister are cooking, but there isn't an ingredient on earth stenchy enough to overpower the flaming wrap.

She opens one eye. A hole has emerged. She torches to the count of ten, then shoves hedge clippers inside the smolder and punches the handles together. The blades won't tear the stretchy black ecto-skin. The stuff is extra terrestrial. Fire, it seems, is the only option.

But it's a bad option. There's ramifications. She blows away smoke and can see that she's scorching the hood. Sure, it can be sanded, painted, then resold, but the windshield will be a different story. Ditto the undercarriage.

"What," Avery says, "is that smell?"

Her sister looks ridiculous in an apron. Pegs reconsiders

what qualifies as ridiculous when she removes her goggles and immediately tears up. The smell infects her.

"You're going to suffocate," Avery says. She dumps laundry in the washer, but hangs onto a shirt and covers her face with it. "Whose car is that?"

"Go cook." Pegs wipes her eyes, coughs. She asks if it's raining. Before Avery can respond, Pegs lifts the garage door a foot. She kneels and chugs air. It isn't surging. It's just rain.

"Just open the door," Avery says. "Unless you stole this from Revo. Then don't."

Pegs slams the door. She stands, shakes her nose left a few times. She lies to her sister, saying the car is just a car, it's normal, it's not from Revo.

Avery looks at the roof. She knows that a Revo car would have a lidar helmet on top. She does not know that the lidar helmet has been removed by a breakdown crew. "I don't believe you," Avery says.

"Are we eating when Dad's home or tomorrow?"

"Do you read what we text you?"

Pegs doesn't say no. She doesn't say that her phone has been clogged with inquiries—the drivers want updates, the Revo app says she's not on pace to hit her surge hours, Dellinger says a RedGill has a dirty helmet. She kneels on a gurgling drain. It's unclear how exactly water is moving underneath her. It feels like she and Avery are riding on a houseboat.

Her sister steps toward the smell. "Are you okay?"

"I'm just thinking. Go cook," Pegs says. "Actually, is there a cookie pan?"

It takes some trial and error to get the metal pan between the car and the wrap. But the pan: the pan is perfect.

She slides it beneath her target spot. She blasts the wrap without scorching the hood. She scoots the pan as she climbs, though twice, she needs a rubber mallet to coax it along. Once, the pan scrapes the hood.

These are problems she's willing to live with after twelve hours without removing a single part. She burns a safe trail up the windshield before realizing that it would've been quicker to go the hamburger way, door to door. The car rocks when she stands on the roof. She finds herself surfing. She grabs the long fluorescent strip light, but quickly lets go—its screws are visible. Too visible. They're small and old. She balances, torch in hand. Clothes spin violently in the washer.

Slowly, she lays the torch on the hood. She breathes, then jumps off. She lifts the garage door, lugs more sandbags inside, and wedges a fresh one against each side of each tire. She adds parts from broken kitchen chairs. She kicks the elliptical up the bumper's ass like a mutant pitchfork.

The rest of the roof goes smoothly. She fires the torch from one knee, then two. Sweat pours off her arms and head onto the black wrap. It evaporates in the heat. The car that appears beneath the membrane looks violated, though not by her. The breakdown crew was rough in their removal of the lidar and rack. It's like looking at some naked thing, not quite a skeleton, but a kind of absence, a white scarring that, even though she's almost five feet off the ground, gives her the sensation of walking under-ground in a graveyard.

When she climbs down and starts on the trunk, she's drenched. Weather of some kind ruffles the door. Perhaps it's the sound of rain, or the perfect rectangularity of the garage, but as she fires the torch she feels like she's in an aquarium. The wind is tapping her glass. Maybe the wind is the filter. Maybe she should focus on what she's actually doing. She should definitely be wearing fire retardant sleeves, but she's too close to the end to stop. She torches all the way to the rear key slot, then yanks the rubber cover down off the trunk. She pulls, stretches, and jerks the black wrap down over the tires. The car is visible. From behind the trunk, it looks brand new. There are no dents, no rust. The gray compact shines under the low lights. If you ignore the left headlight and the scars the breakdown crew left on the roof, it's a perfect-looking car. She has never gutted a frame this good. It's insane. It's insane how she can see the car's attractive qualities and Revo can't. Revo values its tech to such an absurd, secretive degree, yet they don't seem to realize that cars are themselves tech. Revo rips off everything electronic, balls up the car in black wrap, and yet here it is, liberated, pristine, and available for use—one hundred percent fine. It is highly guttable, at any rate. It is attractively, profitably strippable. Pegs sits on the dry concrete, sweat leaving her, air swapping in and out of her lungs, and for the first time, she's foolish enough to let her guard down, thinking: this will work, this is brilliant.

KNOCK KNOCK, TAKE TWO

THE AFTERNOON flies. It doesn't feel as though Pegs is destroying a car. She is isolating value and rescuing it from its cumbersome housing. She even finds a kind of value in the cumbersome parts. The hood is heavy, dented, and now burned, and she lays it in front of the dryer as a container for everything else. She does the same with the floor mats. The front bumper is too damaged to come off clean. The one headlight will definitely sell. Same with the side skirts, which she hadn't factored into her financial estimations.

She takes three- and four-second breaks between each item she liberates from the car. There's no need to pause, calculate, plan, worry. She just…works. She wonders if she is the first person who has ever done this, i.e. removed a futuristic wrap with limited tools. She is definitely the first person to realize that all the wire-housing holes shot through random parts like the headliner will compromise the sales value of an AV gut job. She pictures some cold robotics lab, a lonely university, twenty years ago. A man, to another man: *Imagine trying to resell this car after we've shot wires through every piece.*

She doesn't actually know if the holes in the gauge cluster are AV-related. She doesn't know if Lester will want parts with odd trenches and pits. He could finagle a way to conceal the blemishes from customers. She could conceal them from Lester.

Avery yells down—the laundry, did it buzz, did you switch it. Pegs says she did, then she does. The dryer catapults zippers at its own walls while Pegs counsels herself. The problems she is encountering are the sorts encountered by pioneers. She hears it at work all the time:

It's not a problem, *per se, it's just new.*

The hood fills quickly. She starts storing parts on the washer. She enlists Avery's laundry basket and reminds herself that she's attempting to sell parts backwards through time, from driverless cars to standard ones. Of course there will be issues.

One big issue: she works so effectively on her own, yet she's so rarely alone. Driving doesn't count. She means alone doing work work, hands work. In her parents' garage, she doesn't have to make small talk with non-ops staff, text with drivers, haggle with Lester. It's so much easier to focus. She can adapt her approach on the fly without telling a single nebby soul. No justifications, no fights. No incoming calls on the driverless console screen. She doesn't explain why she decides to pause her interior excavation to unbolt the charging hatch, which is used, obviously, but perfectly good, and as she carries it to the evolving junkyard on the floor, she thinks: I left Lester's then said yes to driving and ultimately stealing because more money is the only way to construct yourself a safe space in this city. She finds herself feeling envious of her father's dry garage, his singular focus, which is also hers, genetically. The place is a sub-level, yet no water gets in. There's caulk in every crack. There's special drainage at the base of the driveway, plus extra drains in the floor, just in case. He didn't half-ass it with tires and plywood on glassblock like Pegs did. The man worked, saved, set himself a task, built a system. He constructed a space where he can exist without worrying about a surge. She has no idea what the weather is doing.

Her sister calls down: are they dry? The clothes are not. Pegs adds twenty minutes. She tries to think of where she could build herself a space like her father's garage. She would need money. She would need to figure out how to exist as a new and necessary middle cog in some car-related process, a cog that functions independently even more so than she does at Revo. She stands still above a drain and tries to picture it: instead of her sister calling down about laundry, a driverless car company will call her company cell phone to…repurpose their used prototypes. She could convert AV parts into normal-V parts.

Or: she can modify certain AV parts into other AV parts.

Maybe there's an angle with collectors.

Or historians.

There's no doubt a way to frame the whole thing environmentally, a kind of waste reduction: P.E.G.S. Auto: Proper Environmental Galopy Salvation.

It's possible that *galopy* is spelled with a *j*. It's a hundred percent possible that none of the AV companies would want their products framed as lemons.

She wraps a side mirror in her mother's red fabric and tells herself she can figure out the next step. Leah has so often told her some version of: you're the only one who can figure out how to connect all these mechanical worlds. It's true. Leah couldn't have figured out a method to safely torch the rubber wrapping. Anna might know more about power inverters and converters and all the electrical power control unit crap, but she couldn't detach it all as neatly as Pegs. The way to reroute her life suddenly feels clear: she needs to isolate herself and her skills. She needs to get rid of Lester, and the drivers, and the programmers like Stomanovich and Boltz, who don't know her name or actual skills. She doesn't even know if they're programmers. They could be engineers. They could be professional ping-pong players for all she knows. The point is that she doesn't need them. What she needs is to harness their ability to pivot. She'll think of some better idea than Wheel or Trav or whatever company they're dreaming up. She'll do it on her own. With others, she gets distracted. She gets angry. Anna always wants things to move slower. Leah wants to speedily collaborate with the whole world minus the people she hates.

Pegs nestles weather strips and taillights in the laundry basket. She stares down at the collection. The parts do not form some kind of slogan for a new company. They don't form an arrow pointing in any particular direction. Teeny heater hoses stick out of the basket's thatching like wings on a chubby spaceship. She pictures the laundry basket floating backward through time. She can see it floating down the carpeted stairs to her apartment. The stolen coffee cone would sniff it, beep, turn. In the kitchen, Pegs crouches over the contents. Her past self would hopefully make some smart interpretation about what the delivery means and what to do and how to pivot, reroute, go, now. She would see the path forward—how to hustle and operate solo, like the girl in the bowling alley, but how to do so without being jerked around by a CounterCash, cleaning up spills, hiding in side rooms, sleeping in them during shelter alerts. She would weaponize her hustle in the name of actually acting on her ideas and brilliant impulses rather than just brainstorming new futures like Boltz or Stomanovich, who hustle, but only intellectually. It's possible this is too much burden to put on a laundry basket. Realistically, if her past self received a basket of parts, she wouldn't waste time interpreting its arrival. She'd try to sell them, pronto.

There's a knock on the garage door. She removes her goggles. The dryer swirls. No other knock follows. The garage door doesn't rise.

Slowly, she traces the GreenGill toward the garage door. The knock isn't her mother or sister, who are already upstairs. Her father wouldn't knock. He'd go straight in, through the front. She walks right to the garage door, sets her ear against it. Without thinking, she taps. There's a response, to her left. It's three taps. It's human.

Pegs holds her breath. There's no record of her parents' address in Revo's system. She has been careful to never input the address during test drives. She briefly wonders why she has behaved this way. Did she know this would one day happen? More likely, she didn't want her mother to see her in the neighborhood, how could you, our daughter, who never tells us anything, driving past, two blocks away, with your fancy car.

There's a human voice outside. The person is speaking through the drainage system. It's echoing up through the floor, like the concrete is speaking. She crouches over a drain. She hears: "Pegs."

She lifts the door to her knees. There's an army of red galoshes outside, dozens. Pegs lifts the handle higher. The galoshes are Leah's, reflecting in the puddles.

Leah crawls under the door. The smell inside staggers her. She tells Pegs to air the place out. Pegs lowers the door to the ground as quietly as she can. When she turns, Leah is circling the prototype. It looks like a roasted chicken carcass Pegs and her sister picked at for two days and then forgot about on the second shelf behind some egg noodles.

Leah kicks a back tire. "Why are these tires on?"

"We've got to tow the frame somewhere."

"So you're done?"

"Watch the torch." Pegs carries it to safety. *Safety* is defined as *what's left of the trunk.* Leah says it all looks done, great. "Looks killer" is what she actually says, not that she'd have any idea. She kneels by the upside-down hood stacked sleigh-like with parts and runs her newly healed, sling-free hand through them with a kind of gentle curiosity, as though they're a litter of newborn farm animals she intends to ferry from a dangerous pen to some safer environment where they can do the dumb repetitive stuff farm animals do. Leah eyes the parts on the floor mats, the laundry basket. She pinches the black wrap. She asks if Pegs skinned a scuba diver.

"God, it sucked," Pegs says. "But we can toss it over everything once we pack a car."

Leah lifts some light, ornately-wrapped object. She catches the rear view mirror when it unfurls. "This fabric is worth at least half what's inside it."

"I want that wrapped."

"People pay for fabric," Leah says. "They pay double with all the supply issues."

On her black greasy fingers, Pegs outlines reasons for using the fabric to wrap parts The glass splinters easily. Plus, they still have to load everything into the tow out on her parents' nosy street. Lester might wind up with some of the stuff in his house, which will drive him nuts, he'll want it hidden, and also—

"We got another," Leah says. She sits on the concrete by the smallest drain. Her boots are full of water. She empties them through a grate.

Pegs says, "Another?" She says the word like she's re-pronouncing the Latin name of a cancer she's just been tagged with.

"A Ryde prototype wrecked." Leah rolls off her damp socks. She opens the dryer and adds the socks to Avery's load. "It got tossed in the surge. A little after Anna." Leah pulls ineffectually at the dryer's 'go' button. She presses the button, turns, points at what's left of the GreenGill. "How soon can we get this out of here?"

In her mind, Pegs can see herself arguing. It's not hard to envision. She can see the entirety of the next hour—bil-lyclubbing her gloves and goggles against her palm, mak-ing stances, gesturing with the torch in a casually threat-ening way. She and Leah pace around the car. They choose places to stand, faces to make. Leah plows onward to new points of contention as though some invisible judge in a skeleton mask is granting her victories, waving the show-down onward to new annoying topics. That's how it goes with Leah. A movie called *Leah Gives Up* would show a title card, then ending credits. There wouldn't be a single filmed moment.

Pegs walks to the washer. She props the passenger's seat against the see-through door. She sits. It feels good to do so. Her legs ache with joy. The idea of fighting doubles the gravity in the garage. It triples the friction. She doesn't feel like explaining how freaking hard the torch and cookie pan was, how she didn't have hose clamp pliers, how dumb it is to steal with strangers from a different driverless company, particularly when the only information Leah seems to know about them is what mask they wear while protesting for better surge pay. She drops the arm rest and says: "No."

"We've got to start scaling this," Leah says.

"This was a nightmare." Pegs crosses her legs, props her arms. Her feet shiver looking at Leah's bare toes on the concrete.

"It'll be faster with help," Leah says.

"I need less people, not more."

"The sector is imploding," Leah says. The dryer blares. Leah adds time and recounts her morning at Revo, postwreck. It had been tense. Everyone in the garage was projecting about as much enthusiasm as a sympathy card. Two vehicles lost before Thanksgiving: not good. When Leah was leaving for her test drive, Yabner started yelling. He was yelling at someone. The person had asked Yabner to be a reference.

"It's the same story at Ryde," she says. "They want our help."

"They want my playbook." Pegs wonders how dirty her jeans are. She is potentially ruining the seat. She recrosses her legs.

"We get half," Leah says.

"I'm split fifty ways right now."

There's a voice upstairs—who is that, who's here, Janice? Her mother says her father is going to murder her if she keeps opening the garage door to that wet driveway.

"Whose crazy car is outside?" her mother asks. "There's a crowd. Bring up an applesauce."

12

YER DEER

IN THE BASEMENT, Pegs grabs a mason jar of applesauce. Up in the kitchen, she hands it to her mother, ignoring the inquiries about the robot car out there, whose is it, when will she move that tow, the longer it sits there, the more likely one of the McGarrity's asks to borrow it, or they'll just take it.

Pegs exits the kitchen, but it's hard to really ever escape in her parents' house. The first floor is a kitchen and living room, front of house and back, end of tour. Her sister tells her again to shut the basement door, it smells horrid downstairs. Pegs responds by kneeling on the couch. She peeks through the front window, the one her father has reinforced from the outside with three sheets of clear plexiglass. She debates unlocking the gun cabinet. Carrying a .22 out into the front yard would be a good way to scare off all the neighbors. They're swarming Leah's Blue-Gill. An entire football game has paused to marvel at it. Uncles and dads with nephews and sons all wear hats in the November dampness. One guy actually puts his hand on a small shoulder. It's as though he's about to turn the kid away from the scene, stricken, like the tow truck and driverless car are two alley cats that have decided to screw right there on the street. Pegs can just see the neighbors, gossiping:

You's see that robot-car on Thanksgiving eve? How about that racket in the Pegula's garage? And that tow. Channel 2 says there's been robo wrecks. Those cars need regulated, I'm telling you, it's fishy and then some, that oldest Pegula has always been a schemer.

Pegs departs her nervy daydream thanks to Leah. It turns out that inviting herself to the Pegula residence was an insufficiently bold move; Leah has now invited herself upstairs, too, bare feet and all. She points her key fob at the window. The alert sounds, the crowd scatters, and Leah begins assessing every square inch of the living room. She can't get enough. She touches the drapes, streaks her pointer down the glass gun cabinet. She laughs at the family pictures on the side table. The poses are ridiculous. In one, Pegs and her sister lean against green marble in white altar serving robes as though they're modeling for *Sexy Catholic Kids Weekly*. Leah is downright bewitched by the antlers above the kitchen doorway. It's a big ten-point rack. The horns are brown, the skull white like melted wax.

Pegs' mother appears beneath the antlers. She carries a box of raspberry Danish Twist. The filling is about the same color as her maroon bathrobe. Her hair is the same short length as Pegs' but in a completely alternate style.

"This is Leah," Pegs announces. "She's just stopping by."

Her mother points upstairs, shushes. "Let your father sleep." She eyes Leah, the Revo rain jacket, her blank toenails. "Are those feet what smells like death downstairs?"

"The socks," Leah says, "were worse."

Marcia Pegula sets the Danish on the square wooden

table in the living room. She sits with her back to the kitchen. She tells Pegs: "I wish you'd told me someone was coming." The woman looks like she has been delivered unimaginably bad news. It's like she's been told Pegs died underneath the car that's polluting her garage. She tells Pegs to at least get waters for everyone, but Pegs does not move toward the kitchen. She creeps toward the front window, spying on the BlueGill from behind the drapes. Two boys are back. They puppy around the car's hood. Pegs tells Leah to trigger the alarm and her mother says: Let them look. Pegs asks why the kids aren't in school. Her mother says remote day, morning surge, plus it's already four, you've worked all day, you're insane.

"What's insane," Avery says, "is Dad getting called in for tonight but kids can't be at school to learn." Avery emerges from the kitchen with waters. Carrying three glasses at once: ridiculous. Her white apron: even more ridiculous.

"The kids learn," their mother tells Avery. "The district spends a fortune on wireless hotspotters."

"Ours would cut out," Leah says, "all the time."

Leah explains that she means in college, not high school, she's not that young. Pegs' mother offers no interest, sympathy, or eye contact. As soon as Pegs and Leah sit with her at the table, she tells Pegs: "Go get another chair. Your father will be up soon."

"She's just stopping by," Pegs says.

"It's not a crime to share," her mother says. She circles a hand above the Danish. "Eat it all."

Leah consults the doorway antlers re: whether eating an entire pan of Danish is polite. Her concern then shifts to Marcia Pegula, who produces a bullet from her bathrobe. It's lipstick. She taps the wooden table. "We do our

Thanksgiving on Wednesday. My husband has to be at the store."

"How long have you had the store?"

"We don't own Macy's, hon."

Pegs hates *hon*. Despises it. Between her mom with *hon* and her sister's stupid apron, it's like the Pegula women have decided to playact as diner waitresses from the previous century. Leah seems so modern in contrast. She sips her water across from Pegs and tells Marcia that her family doesn't even eat together on Thanksgiving anymore. They do it in January, sometimes February, depending on how long surges last. Marcia Pegula inquires about the fifth chair, where is it, did her daughter break an ankle, is she deaf. Pegs informs her that there may in fact be some chair-related issues in the garage. Some broke. She needed them. As…padding. Her mother asks: Is that all the noise? The chairs?

"Did you make those drapes?" Leah asks Marcia Pegula.

"They did not make themselves."

"Talented family," Leah says.

Pegs genuinely cannot believe that Leah is at her parents' wooden table assessing her family's talent level. She can't believe Leah drove here, then came upstairs, dripping wet, shoeless. Pegs still cannot believe Leah wants her to work on a second car, from Ryde, now, here. It is a genuine miracle that Leah did not bring along Ryde drivers to her parents'. Pegs looks out at the BlueGill. No one is sitting in the front or back.

"Pegs is the most talented person I know," Leah says.

Marcia Pegula repeats the name with disdain: *Pegs*. Leah looks at her as though she's worried the robed hilltop woman is hiding a third shotgun in her robe. Leah

takes and eats Danish slowly. It's like she expects to discover a bone.

Pegs drinks her water. "Leah," she says, "is a bad influ-
ence."

Her mother asks, "Bad how?"

Leah holds her little Danish in fingers from each hand.
She addresses Pegs, first with a look, then: "I get that your
whole philosophy is 'paddle hard and alone' or whatever." Leah bites, chews. "But some things cannot be boot-
strapped."

Pegs comes very, very close to dismissively repeating the
phrase *whole philosophy*. It's possible she mouths part of it.
It's possible her mother repeats the phrase without Pegs
fully hearing it. "Your thing has bad written all over it,"
Pegs says.

Marcia Pegula: "What thing?"

Pegs asks her mother for privacy. Her mother says sure,
I'll polish the chandeliers in the Southern Sitting Room.
Her slippers clap into the kitchen, where she criticizes Avery's potato mashing. Leah guides the shallow Danish box
around the waters. The huge sheet is cut into rectangles
with a kind of laser precision that suggests some kind of
Revo tool was involved. Pegs doesn't even want one. But
they're just so pluckable the way they're isolated.

Pegs chews, listening in on the kitchen—faucet, arguing,
bottle opener. Quietly, she asks Leah how many people are
involved from Ryde.

"Sounds like five," Leah says. "Plus you, me, and Anna."

Pegs can't help herself: "Five?" She tries to differentiate
herself from her reiterative mother; she does so by theat-
rically raising five Danish-glazed fingers. She tells Leah
that she just gutted the the car all by herself. Five is too

many. It's pointless. It's more risk, less profit. There's not enough for everyone to do.

"We'll find roles," Leah says.

Pegs sets her Danish on the wood table. She clasps her hands to the right of it. "I'm the only one who actually does the work," she says. "There. Said it."

Leah eyes the kitchen, the antlers. "You act like it's this impossible thing to work with people," she says.

"The world is not this big *kumbaya*," Pegs says.

"Exactly," Leah says. "It's horrible, which is why you can't just abide by all these old ideas and expect different outcomes."

Pegs flicks her Danish like a penny—once for "old," once for "ideas." Each time, it spirals half a loop, stops. She envisions Leah's blonde head on the table, spinning. She envisions shoving the Danish and waters across the table and into her rain jacket. Pegs breathes. "I'm not that much older than you."

"The longer you ignore how bad things are, the longer you put off doing what's necessary."

"None of this is *necessary*." Pegs wants to focus on her fight with Leah, but she can only focus on how all she does is repeat words. It's such a stupid tic. The stupid house reprograms her brain. It casts a spell the second she's on the property. She becomes less like herself and more like… them. More specifically: *her*. She counsels herself to be her own distinct person. She will exhibit carefully chosen brilliant habits and speech patterns. She thinks of words that have not been said. She does not think anyone has said the word *risky* thus far. She could say "It's too risky," but she knows Leah will just reply: you're driving cars in surges, wake up, we're at risk every day.

Leah drinks. She taps her nails on the table. It's more than tapping. She looks intent on carving a message into the wood, one she won't revise or retreat from. "I want to get more money for more people however I can."

Pegs eats. "I prefer this."

"We're down to just the two of us driving."

"I'm fine being patient and waiting for Lester to sell this new stuff," Pegs says. "Sue me."

Leah stares. She holds it. She's steady. "You're the one who came to me about Lester."

"You caught me in the supply room."

"You were obsessed about moving parts," Leah says. "You had a whole plan."

"That was parts."

Her mother calls to them from the kitchen: "Your father."

They sit in silence with their Danish and waters. Blue-Gill4 is drawing a fresh crowd. There's now a woman or two. Older kids throw a football above the lidar helmet. Adults aren't even telling them not to. Fuzzy-eared Frank O'Neill from the street over lurks on the fringes. He's got one hand in his coat pocket. It is menacing and then some. He parts the kids. From his jacket he extracts an object that shines in the sunless evening. He measures the lidar frame with a tape measure.

Pegs crosses the room more urgently than she wants to. She bangs on the window. Nine heads turn in unison. She shoos the group. She stands on the couch in an attempt to peek down and ensure that the sloping driveway is empty. It appears to be childless, spyless, though she can't see all the way to the sandbags.

Avery hangs her apron on a chair back, sits, and plucks a

Danish. "I bet Revo would be mad if they saw you scaring off all their free PR."

"Nothing about that car is free," Pegs says.

"It's like a spaceship," their mother says. She loiters beneath the antlers, a pagan priestess assessing a galactic threat.

Leah raises the keys. "If you want, you can drive it."

"She cannot drive it," Pegs says.

"I thought the whole point," Avery says, "is that no one drives it."

"Hey mom," Pegs says, "ask Avery how much she's been putting toward our rent."

Leah breaks up the bickering with an update from her phone. Anna, it seems, would appreciate an update. She wants to know how things are going. Marcia sits and asks if they'll need a chair for this Anna person.

"The whole company is coming," Pegs says. She joins the three women at the table. "Any minute."

Avery laughs. It's fake laughter. She says the crazy car people would never come here. "They're probably all on some island for the holiday weekend."

"They'll work all night," Leah says. "Guaranteed."

"Don't they have families?" her mother asks. "It's criminal. They should be home."

"Dad hunted," Avery says. "Every year."

"Not on Thanksgiving."

"I know a hunting joke," Leah says.

Pegs' mother: "Hunting *is* a joke."

"So this guy is talking to Saint Peter in heaven," Leah says, "and Peter says: you've got an IQ of 200. Go down to room 101, they're working on the Middle East."

"A mess over there," their mother says.

Avery: "Well..."

"A second guy comes in with an IQ of 180, and Saint Peter says: great, go to room 100, we've got people on world hunger."

"If Saint Peter knows what's good for him, there'll be no children in my room," Marcia Pegula says. "I'm a school nurse," she tells Leah in an entirely different voice, one that Pegs had been hoping for, albeit earlier. It's a hammy voice that's got hours of kid-puke stories to tell.

"So the third guy comes in, IQ 80," Leah says. "And Saint Peter leans forward, and he says: did ya get yer deer?"

All three women laugh. Polite laughter, genuine laughter, big cheap laugher—it's a mix. Pegs finds herself softening. She never allows herself to feel soft around Leah. She's always bracing, preparing counterarguments, inhaling. She watches Leah eat her third or fourth Danish and thinks: I talk to her more regularly than any other single person, save maybe Lester. She doesn't actually know much about Leah. Leah lives outside the city. She's younger. She protests. Red rain boots.

It's possible, Pegs thinks, that Leah comes from people who hunt. She is potentially of rural, humble stock. It's very possible—likely, even—that Leah experiences Pegs' exact same recipe of skepticism, worry, and ambition, and that she does so on a daily basis. It's possible that Leah, too, is trying to break from certain routines and habits and genes. She doesn't know the girl's inner calculus. It's impossible to tell what's a pose or a conviction or a sincere experiment. It's not as though Pegs has ever once asked her directly: what's your town like? Your family? Tell a joke. Maybe she's full of them. Maybe she's really, really funny. Maybe all the protestors and Ryde drivers confide in her and trust her because she can tell deer jokes. More likely, it's because she pays attention. To people. She notices how people are and what they need. She can adjust herself to their altitude, yet she also has a special, distinct, distinguishable point of view honed during what seems to have been a very specific childhood and adolescence full of sequential social failures which demonstrated that the long stone path the city laid out before her was positively wrecked with deep cracks. Somehow she learned or decided or perhaps instinctually knew that locking arms would ensure no one, herself included, ever lost themselves down the holes that opened up with alarming frequency.

Pegs' mother squints at her phone. She returns it to her robe. "The weather says an hour until an alert. Can you stay for dinner?"

Leah nods. Pegs is told again to fetch a chair. "The chairs are not super safe at the moment," she says.

"Safe?" her mother says. "What, are they past inspection?"

"I've got to get back to work," Pegs says, to which her mother replies: "It's no crime for us to add a seat."

20

AFTER THE five of them eat, her mother says: stay and visit. No one does. Leah wants to leave before the rain becomes a surge. Avery has dishes, their father has work. Lester texts about the tow, he's looking out back, funny thing, no tow.

Pegs backs Leah's BlueGill down the slope. She parks at the sandbags. When she raises the garage door, Leah is sliding into her socks, her red galoshes. Together, they disentangle the driver's door from the elliptical.

"Who would ever need just a door?" Leah says. She lifts it. Pegs joins her.

"At BG Collision," Pegs says, "doors was all they let me do."

Leah steps first over the sandbags into rain. "Their loss."

"I was just a desk girl."

Leah asks if they need to remove the door on the Blue-Gill. It's a thought. It would make loading the backseat easier, but it's also more work. They've done plenty. Pegs opens the back right door and they find the one diagonal angle that will work. They lift and push the driver's door, hard. It slides in the backseat, a perfect close fit. The four green Revo slashes face forward like a jail cell with a decent view.

Leah shoves floor carpeting into the backseat. "Where are we taking what's left of the frame?"

"It can stay a day."

"I told the Ryde people we had garage space for their car."

Pegs whacks Leah's thigh with weather strips. She stuffs the strips in the backseat. "I don't want strangers at my parents'."

"I figured you'd want to work where you're comfortable." Leah jostles the car door riding unbuckled in the back seat. She wiggles the blower motor through a crevice. She adds: "You get so particular. It's hard to predict what you'll want."

"I can work anywhere."

"So where should I have them take the car?"

She wants to say: I do not want the problems of Ryde drivers to be my problems, and therefore think I have decided that I will not be helping them. She revises: "I don't know a single one of these people."

"Every step will be a conversation."

They run out of room in the backseat. More specifically, they run out of items that will be an easy fit, so Leah brings small stray items to the crowded backseat. She drops the hood latch on top of the uneven stack. The pointy metal item Plinko's heavily toward the seat like it's clinking down a short wishing well.

There's barely space for them to drape the exterior black car wrap across the backseat. They yank what they can through the ceiling's grab handles. Her father's hammers make perfect cinches. Leah lifts the detached car door an inch. She stuffs the wrap underneath it, and from the driver's seat, Pegs surveys their efforts at deception. The black shiny backdrop looks decent. It looks like an approximation of night. Sort of. The wrap doesn't stretch all the way to the ceiling. A bowed sliver of light streaks across the top of the rearview mirror. It's as though the car is filled to the roof with dark water. Pegs tries to simulate the perspective of the driver monitoring system on the dash. It does not look like night, necessarily. It looks like strange shade. "It looks like we're hiding a body," Pegs says.

"No one at Revo is going to be checking the video logs," Leah says. "It was crazy there today. You know what it's like after a wreck."

Leah reclines in the passenger seat. She slides it as far back as it will go. Together, they carry the spare passenger seat away from the washing machine. They flip it upside down and wiggle it like a Tetris block on its twin in the front seat, then they shove as much as they can in the trunk. It fills quickly. Who knew: it's hard to fit a car inside a car. Pegs had been hoping to take more on the first trip to Lester's. It's unclear whether they'll be able to transport the hood. Lester may not even want it. Her father definitely won't want it laying around his garage.

"So should I tell them to bring the car here," Leah says, "or…?"

Pegs lifts a box of bulbs, seat belts, and other miscellany. She hauls it out into the light rain. Leah follows her up the driveway to the tow.

"They need help," Leah says. Pegs replies that she needs help, too—she tells Leah to get the door to the tow. Pegs sets the box on the passenger's seat. It takes up a surprising amount of space. The cab is small. The truck bed is bigger, but it's exposed. Leah asks if there are certain parts that can go in the truck bed.

Pegs bellies over the tow's bedside panel. She cups her hand and scoops water from the truck bed. "We shouldn't risk anything back here tonight."

Leah walks to the tow's license plate. She reaches to the dangling gold hook. It's huge. She pulls. The cable holds. Her pose and expression do not in any way say "save me." They say "I could get used to a life of rescuing." Leah swirls the hook. "I'm helping Ryde with their car."

Pegs shuts the door to the tow. She heads down the slope. "It just gives me a bad feeling," she says.

"We stick to first names," Leah says. "And we never give them our dots. We form the relationship exactly how we want. Skepticism is good. It's important."

"The goal was an apartment," Pegs says. She stalls out on the rest. She doesn't want to say "and I failed." Or: "and now I don't have a plan." She has the sense that any counter she offers up would be true while also being pathetic and insufficient.

"Revo is not forever." Leah says. "You weren't there today, after the crash. They can tell the end is coming."

Their pockets fizz and chirp. They don't need to look. It's a shelter alert. When Pegs hands Leah the keys to the tow, Leah's shock is real. She looks to the roof of the vehicles like she's sizing up a nine-foot security guard who has caught her shoplifting red galoshes. She says she doesn't feel comfortable.

"I need the BlueGill," Pegs says. "I'm behind on hours."

"It's a twenty minute drive."

"Yeah, six times." Pegs doubts they'll make three separate trips. They'll be lucky to complete two. "It looks fishy if I haven't driven."

"No one cares."

"I took a sick day. I said I'd catch up on hours."

"No one is tracking hours." Leah zips her rain jacket. "No one's tracking anything. Every single person at Revo is convinced they're getting fired."

Neither of them can ignore the rain any longer. They raise their hoods. In their gray Revo rain jackets, they look like twins, like smooth, hand-me-down chess pieces whose armor has been sanded down by weather. Leah's shoulders are sharper. She keeps her zipper lower. Before Pegs can further itemize and analyze all their small differences, Leah circles the tow. She climbs into the driver's seat and jiggers the huge wheel. "It's like driving a dumpster."

Pegs closes the passenger's door. She doesn't shut it. She hides in the thin opening. "You okay driving it with that arm of yours?"

Leah nods. "McArdle is closed. You'll have to loop back through the tunnel."

With her hand, Pegs tests the stack of supplies on the floor. It's sturdier than what's on the seat. "How crucial is it for me to help Ryde with their car?"

Leah inserts the key. She turns it gingerly. "It's just a car," she says. "We'll find a video or something."

Pegs tells her to honk until Lester opens. She jogs to the garage and aims the leaf blowers toward the drains. The tow departs. It could be the tow simply idling. It's hard to tell with all the electric-powered air. Pegs holds the garage door above herself like a pull-up bar. The state of things inside isn't too bad, assuming you ignore the gutted car frame, the parts smothering both laundry appliances, the chairs crinkled up like origami at the wall. Water-wise, the place looks decent.

The roads are a different story. She drives through her

parents' neighborhood in manual to ensure the system doesn't log her parents' address, and a surge descends, a real monster. One delivery drone flies, another clutches every steel fingernail to the blue scalp of a mailbox. The BlueGill is noticeably heavy. She rides the wet brake. It strikes her that she's being presented with the precise scenario that automation was created for—you've slept poorly, it's a heavy load, plus generationally bad weather, the kind that just blew a shipping box up into what's left of a dogwood, so how much do you trust yourself, really? Some long whippy thing falls from the backseat—a wiper, a hose. The part rides down the car door in the backseat and clatters on the floor. It's possible the DMS will log the sound. There might be a question about it.

She watches the screen. No one calls from Revo about the clatter. No one calls because the DMS isn't even on. She tells herself: you're driving. At the base of the hill, she parks and initiates the system. It proposes Revo as the destination. She types the laundromat near she and Lester.

BlueGill4 rolls onto Saw Mill Run. It's the lone car looping along the ribbon back toward the city. Tiny lights peek above the black curtain behind her. They rush at the BlueGill and then disappear, late angels hurrying to someone more needy. Delivery drones stream over the windshield. They're so fast in the surge. It's like they know it's getting worse out. She follows them into the long Fort Pitt Tunnel. The system finally gives some good gas. The BlueGill hurtles through the left lane. Another part drops or settles, somewhere in the trunk. She wonders where the hell she'll dump the frame. She'll need Lester's tow. Again. She wonders if she should just do it tonight. The rivers are high. Clean ledges are hard to find.

Perhaps it's a task better suited to the Ryde drivers—if you can get rid of my other frame, I'll strip your car. She should've pitched the idea to Leah. She should've fought a bit more about the whole thing. The whole back-and-forth was unusual. Leah seemed to respect Pegs' decision about not helping the folks from Ryde. Leah didn't push, didn't grandstand.

Pegs looks at herself in the rear view mirror. Her eyes have no lift. Her blinks are gentle. Maybe Leah was taking pity on her. More likely, Leah didn't fight much because Pegs didn't actually make a decision. Not authoritatively, at least. She dodged. She shrank and hid.

The end of the tunnel opens like a mouth. The BlueGill holds at fifty-five every foot of the way. She's near the exit, then at and through it. Wind is waiting on the bridge. The car jostles. The wind is blowing like it's getting paid for every rain molecule it can shove through the bridge's gutters to the Monongahela, fifty feet below. The green directional signs vibrate. Nothing secures their metal bottoms. The BlueGill speeds underneath them, feeling heavy, fast.

The system guides her left into a new lane. It guides her left again, near the barrier. As the bridge ends, she skids. The car takes its time straightening. She hears water, the treads. She can feel every part in the backseat and trunk. It feels like they're on her lap. The system feels them, too. It's still learning how to carry new weight. It's accustomed to a secret load in the trunk, but the extra car door is heavy. The backseat is full. Pegs reaches to her right, testing the upside down passengers's seat. It's sturdy beside her. It kicks forward when the car cruises into the dip off the bridge. The BlueGill speeds out of the trough and climbs toward the Fort Duquesne Bridge.

Then, the car accelerates rapidly. She has rarely felt it

move as though it is being chased. There's no obstacle in the thin channel up to the bridge. There's only water, pouring left and right off downspouts to the shoreline and advancing river. Her side mirror is empty. The passenger mirror is blocked by the Tetris seat. The black wrap fills the rear view.

The BlueGill hits fifty-five. It hits sixty. She reaches for the console screen and switches the view from map to aerial. A small black object grows ten-fold. The black dot swallows the whole screen in the same instant that some sharp metal object strikes the roof. She ducks in her seat. The system brakes, but the vehicle abides by other laws, those of the physical world. It feels as though the car's acceleration continues unabated. The tires scream. The screen does, too, bleating red. Pegs doesn't read the alert. She doesn't need to. She grabs the wheel, pumps the brakes, twice, three times, relentlessly. She drives like she can both straighten the car and shake off whatever object is on her. Nothing has slid down the windshield except heavy rain. Her impulse is to wiggle the car as though she's been bit by a bug still leeching out blood. She can't hear the tires over the rattle in the trunk and backseat, both of which are fishing the car left. She turns that way. She does so violently, her hands throwing the wheel. There's no prayer of straightening. Glass breaks. It's dense glass. It sounds like one femur fracturing another.

The short side wall of the bridge straight ahead of her is not made of glass. It is not broken, except for the wide gutter. She steers away from the concrete wall, but the wall steers toward her. The car doesn't turn. It won't. The wall advances. She aims for the gutter, glances at the edge, and she's through it.

For a second it feels as though the car is spinning so

fast that she'll be able to turn around and see the hole she drove through. Maybe she does. Maybe the car spins seven times in mid-air, mid-surge. All she registers is sky. Every dark cloud plunges into her stomach. She is suffocatingly airborne. She grips the wheel, desperate to straighten the rubber into clock hands she can squeeze and control, freeze, but time speeds. There's no epiphany, no memory flash. Time and her body fly forward. The fall is short. The river blasts through her senses, puncturing them like a needle through five balloons.

The whiteness in her vision fades. The airbag shrinks. The windshield is splintered. It's halfway submerged. She hears hissing. It's behind her. In or out, water air, she can't tell.

Her chest throbs. She grabs at it. She can't reach her ribs. The seat belt is still inflated. It's choking her. She reaches for the door, and her left arm becomes sleeved in fire. Broken, sprained, who knows. Pain is pain. She can't pull the lever. A fist is impossible. Her right arm can't reach the driver's door over the inflatable seat belt. The river wobbles at the window.

She undoes her seat belt and rips off the inflated strap one-handed. She could swear this motion alone sinks her deeper. She tries to move more…calmly. She mashes window buttons. Nothing lowers, except for all of it. The passenger's seat riding shotgun slumps forward as though dead, and Pegs reaches under it. She stretches her good fingers to the door. The lever won't pull. The pressure is too great.

The car rolls. She leaps so hard back into the driver's seat that her shoulder thuds the window. The water has risen. The car dips again, banking forward. Every synapse and neuron fires simultaneously, a self-generated burst of survivalism that boosts her like a rocket toward the backseat, where the side windows are more air than water. But the backseat is packed. And wrapped. The black material is drawn wide. She yanks the top without ripping it. She reaches to the floor. There's a foot of river at the bottom. She can't lift the spare door with one hand. She's at a bad angle. She can't recline for a better one.

The car bobs. It can't decide how it wants to sink. The windshield is fully submerged. It's intact, though. The windshield is not the cause of the water she hears.

She kneels backwards on the driver's seat. The rush of water sounds closer. She reaches around her seat, around the wrap and detached door. She can feel the river's icy flow coming in low through the back window. The window is fractured. Water sloshes on the back seat. She inhales one huge gulp of air as though she's about to plunge. She isn't. Her brain is simply low on oxygen and has decided to have a say. She fills her lungs twice more. As the car plunges, trunk first, she tries to think. The dead passenger's seat collapses backward. It rolls onto the center console. It bears down on the detached door spanning the back, one of countless obstacles that make an escape through the broken rear window impossible. She tries the button on her own window. The door still won't open against the river. She punches the glass with a flat palm, then searches wildly for any hard, swingable item. With the seat belts inflated, the metal tongues won't reach. She snakes her arms into the watery floor of the backseat. Her fingers skim through rubber hoses and weather strips until she feels the metal hood latch beside them, grabs it, and stabs its metal hook into her window, over and over. When she creates a crack, she begins to kick. She raises her knees to her chest and stomps the glass. She unfurls all of her remaining energy through her feet and wastes oxygen on screams until she kicks through to water. Glass tears her pants, her shins. The car inhales the river. Water bobs at the ceiling, then covers her head. She inhales a last breath and then contorts herself through the window. Piercings and scrapes along her hips and shoulders are easy prices to pay for air.

When she emerges in the river, the air is warm, then freezing. She reaches for the car, holds onto the hood while it's at water-level. Small round lights blind her eyes. They're so close. It's as though the roof has grown head-lights. She pushes off the vehicle when she sees the delivery drone, wrapped around the lidar helmet, alive. Its arms dent but don't break the clear shell. The drone stays loyal to its prey as it sinks below the jagged waters. The two lights shine until they disappear.

God does she miss the car. The car was good. It was the best. It was safe. Sure, the car was sinking, and she was trapped, and there were multiple physical objects attempting to kill her, but the car allowed her to exist on the rough surface for a year-long minute. She spasms in the wide river, reaching for a sturdy port. The concrete promenade is seven or eight car-lengths to her left.

Up, her cells scream. Her feet kick at heavy nothing-ness. They have no impact, don't move enough water. She thrusts her head skyward against the wind and rain that force her down, pressing her against the Allegheny like a thumb on an open hose. She gags on the river, drooling coughs. She can't wipe her eyes. Water stings her vision.

Her left arm is useless. Her right paddles, hard. It's like

she's climbing an endless ladder. The only thing saving her from being swallowed is how fast the river moves. She's falling too fast horizontally to fall vertically. The tube of river pushes her, pushes her. After two or three more weak one-handed paddles, the BlueGill is ten car lengths behind her. It's not behind her. It's nowhere. It's gone.

The promenade is disappearing, too. It's shrinking at any rate. There's another block or two of concrete, then she'll be delivered to the middle of a new, huge, wide river. She doesn't swim toward the concrete wall so much as smash her arm out ahead of her, punching the water. She holds her left arm low, numbing it in the river. God it hurts. She yells about it. She grunts as a way to propel herself toward the T-shaped tie-offs. The cement gets higher the closer she gets.

She picks a tie, aims for it, and reaches—but she's pushed past the tie before she can leap. Her arm drags along the scab of asphalt. The sharp concrete bite is short-lived—she falls to the water, and for the first time since kicking through the window, she goes fully under. She kicks, convulses. She pops, inhales.

She's got eight, maybe ten more ties to go. She can see where the Allegheny becomes the wide Ohio, which flows to the Mississippi, the Gulf, the world. She wriggles out of her Revo rain jacket. Her lungs take on water. She holds the strong fabric above the river. Water spills from the hood.

At the next tie, she reaches for the concrete with her right. Her limp left drops the rain jacket near the tie. It doesn't catch. She falls. The effort of retrieving the jacket sends her backward into the river, face toward the sky, then underwater.

She stays there.

Some stray bit of trash strikes her leg. It could be a tree branch. A dead hard fish. The impact of it shoots frozen blood through her southern veins. Her legs are jolted into writhing aliveness. She's terrified by the thought of all the bloodless objects in the river. Being dragged down is a more horrifying thought than simply drowning, and so she cups her hands. She pulls her scarred body upward, toward air, just in time to see a tie-off pass. There's three or four left. There could be twenty. She can barely see through water and fear. The top of her heart feels frozen. The bottom beats very fast, like it's trying to squeeze blood through an eye dropper to her entire body. She reaches to the cement. She holds the ledge. She tests her left—she can't make a fist.

In one motion, she lifts herself higher. She reaches the jacket to the tie. The hood catches. She slides down it like a fire pole, and her hands find a pocket. She squeezes. In her mind, she crawls inside.

She stays like that, holding onto the jacket. The pocket fills with water. When her hand aches, she reaches her left arm up to a sleeve and hooks her wrist inside. She bobs against the concrete, a broken bent scarecrow with its elbow above its head. She needs one hundred breaths before she can climb. Maybe a thousand. The ledge is high.

She counts ten breaths. Bottles and paper and formless murk float past at five and ten miles an hour. She stares across the Allegheny to the cement walk on the other side. It feels about as achievable as the cement right above her. The teeny waves splash her chattering teeth. They paint her throat. Her pulse lives in her left wrist.

A fast heaviness glances her ankle. It grabs at her, then

is gone. She beats her shoes so hard against intruders that she pops above the surface. She falls hard, stretching the jacket. The visitor had been formidable. She can't see it. She can't see her own waist in the water. She sweeps her legs like torches scaring nocturnal water demons, kicking at random. She tells herself that the car would've scared off any living creature. The BlueGill was heavy, violent. It's a world away, upstream and way down.

Rain hits her, hard. She has not registered it until now. She opens her mouth to breathe. White breath rolls out of her like sleepy smoke, and she calls out, screaming. She hasn't seen a boat in weeks. It's possible that she has stopped paying close attention. She imagines herself at home, the shower cold, then hot. She thinks of eating. She thinks of her stomach never again knowing food. The current hits her and hits her. She pictures the waves smacking her then circling the world and returning to hit her harder, full of scraps from their journeys. She braces against each wave. She stops bracing. The jacket squeaks in her hand. She's sliding.

But Pegs—like the Revo rain jacket, like the membranic car wrap—is made of strong, strange stuff. She holds on. She doesn't climb. She can't. It's too high. Her wrist is too weak, so she breathes. She breathes more. She breathes in and out for so long that, over at Lester's, Leah becomes worried. She opens her phone. She stares at Pegs' dot in the app. It does not blink. It communicates *Last Signal* via a solid, static orange circle. It's hard to tell whether the dot is at the Fort Duquesne Bridge or the promenade beneath it. Leah drives the tow over grass and around crash poles at Point State Park. She drives with the high beams lit then walks to the river on foot in the rain. Leah yells, wanders. She hears her own name being shouted then sees her, below the ledge. Leah hoists Pegs out, and at the ER, all Pegs can look at is her wrist. Like the car sinking in the river, the bruise looks like black edgeless mold on a blue-gray cloud. Leah rubs her shoulders. She rubs more. When Leah speaks, she says: you made it further than the car. The nurse is more interested in Pegs' bloody pants than her wrist. The nurse wants to know: has she been assaulted? The non-ops staff at Revo want to know if they can draw Revo slashes on the cast. Revo wants Pegs to take a few days, then provide a statement as they pursue damages from the drone people, but two days later, her meeting gets canceled. In the wake of the third wreck, all of Revo gets canceled. *Delivery,* the CEO's email says, *is truly the life-blood of the country, which is why we're partnering with FR8.* Half the company and every driver then receives an HR email—they'll be paid through November and December. Leah uses her severance on a rundown brick rental unit in Dormont starting 12/1. When she invites Pegs to come see it, Pegs falls asleep on the bus, then the T. There's already a handful of visitors waiting for her in the detached garage. They're standing around a six-wheel prototype from Ryde. The windshield is shattered.

"Is this an intervention?" Pegs says. A woman with green glasses asks about Pegs' arm, the cast, it must be hard keeping it dry. Pegs tells Leah that it's deeply unfair to be put on the spot like this. Leah says: I'll pay for your time.

Pegs does not allow this. She instructs two of the women and the one man re: where to stand. When watching a team of strangers attack the car on her command, she feels inspired. This feeling is quickly cut with guilt. She did not choose alliance. She agreed to work alongside others only when she couldn't do the work herself. She watches other hands trigger impact wrenches on the doors of a second Ryde car and has the awful sense that she has chosen the right route but done so for the wrong reason and at far too late a juncture. She embraced these opportunities only out of desperation, not belief.

Leah's response to these kinds of self-reflections: *Would you cut yourself a break? You survived a fall off a bridge.*

She curses herself hoarse when Lester says he doesn't want their parts anymore, too much drama, can't risk it, too many outsiders. Anna finds them a new buyer in Ohio. Pegs immediately regrets the meeting she takes with Boltz and Stomanovich. They and the other gadgeteers at their new office want Pegs involved somehow. It mostly seems like they just don't want her to go work with Dellinger or Yabner on whatever project Dellinger or Yabner are now doing. Pegs never quite understands what Boltz and Stomanovich are doing. Scooters, automated delivery, who knows. Boltz keeps saying a robust testing period will commence as soon as surges end, but surges persist to January. February's clouds are filled with crud. The girl from the bowling alley isn't working the night Pegs drives there, her arm healed. The shoe system is fully automated. The CounterCash addresses Pegs by her jacket color. It asks: "What size?"

Some days, it feels like she truly knows her shape. She fills a specific role in an evolving complex system of pseudo-theft in which the remaining driverless car companies are too sacred to publicize their failures, and so Leah, Pegs, and others deftly acquire these embarrassing vehicles. Other days it feels imperative that Pegs grow, that she somehow inflate herself into some sturdier-seeming person so that if she were to ever track down the girl from the bowling alley, the girl would think: this Pegs person is a rock. On many days, money feels dire. The kitchen window keeps leaking. Surge pay is an insufficient replacement for severance. Leah tells her to actually do something about it, but when the bus approaches the protest, there are only four attendees on the sidewalk. Pegs wishes there were more. There's no Leah yet. The bus idles at the red light before the stop. Pegs doesn't know what number she needs to see on the sidewalk to feel comfortable leaving the bus. She has a hard time picturing herself in a group without Leah. She makes a fist around the yellow stop cord. She debates pulling it, how hard, when. She waits to see if someone else will do it first. Her arm is the only one that's raised. Her elbow stays high. She scans the seats, waiting for another arm to beat her to it.

All of these inner dilemmas would happen, but only after minutes or hours or days in the dark river, debating: climb or breathe? The rain picks up. Her shoes weigh her down. She kicks them off. She pictures the BlueGill spotting them—it rolls backward or maybe forward three muddy feet so the shoes can land on the low wet earth. She has no idea how deep a river is. She can't remember which direction the car was facing when it sank. She looks at the bridge and gasps. She shudders. The bridge is so tall.

She squeezes the jacket tighter. She yells. She can't tell if it's surging or raining. The force against her feels ten times more powerful than the one from above. Then again, there's more of her in the river. It's insurmountably endless. A uni-cellular spark of hope rattles somewhere amongst all her rib-chilling dread, then, without warning, this granular bright feeling slips between a crack. It exits

her. She feels a kind of helplessness that's like omni-cellu-
lar panic. Her body is a hopeless vehicle. The concrete is so
long on both sides of her. The stadiums are empty across
the shore.

No one is coming except for the river. It keeps hit-
ting her. It's never going to stop. It will outlast her. She
thinks of different poses and places she might be found
in. She has no faith in her ability to float. She tells herself to breathe. Breathing is the only way to live. It's the
only option she has. Nothing useful floats her way. She
breathes and tries to convince herself that rain is good.
Rain is a miracle, a goddamn gift. If it keeps raining, she'll
be lifted out. She counsels herself not to get caught up
in the particulars or the timeline. For years, things have
been happening so much faster than anyone could have
predicted. The thought calms her pulse. She breathes her
calmest breath. It's an incredible relief to know that the
faster everything drowns, the sooner she can rise.

Acknowledgments

In 2019, I received a $4,000 Creative and Performing Arts Grant from the Pennsylvania State System of Higher Education that helped me research and complete this novel. I am grateful for these funds and for the many other benefits I've received from my union, the Association of Pennsylvania State College & University Faculties. It is my hope this book offers proof of what is possible when temporary, contract, and/or adjunct workers receive support.

I also owe thanks to Sinjon Bartel, Qing Qing Chen, Ken Li, Jake Fisher, and Victoria Ketterer for their readerly feedback; to Dan DeWeese for his heroic stewardship of this project and the projects of so many brilliant makers; and, of course, to Candace Jane Opper, for partnering with me in all matters of making, whether the goal be true sentences or full lives or a more just future.

About the Author

Patrick McGinty received his MFA in Fiction from Portland State University. His fiction and essays have appeared in publications including *ZYZZYVA*, *The Baffler*, *Bright Wall/Dark Room*, and *The New Inquiry*, among others. His Sunday book reviews regularly appear in *The Pittsburgh Post-Gazette*, and he teaches in the English Department at Slippery Rock University. He lives in Pittsburgh, Pennsylvania, with his wife, Candace Jane Opper, and their son.